O9-ABF-859

He clasped his hand over hers, the last bite of chocolate hanging between them.

"Take it," she urged.

Her voice was too sexy to ignore. He grabbed her hand and drew it to his mouth. Cade enveloped the chocolate with his mouth and swallowed it down. The motion was both carnivorous and sexual.

Abby's brown eyes widened in surprise.

"What did you expect?" he asked.

"I don't know," she said. "Something more…"

"Polite?" he asked.

Her eyes darkened. "Maybe. If so, I'm glad I was wrong."

His gut tightened. "You need to be careful. You're asking for trouble."

"Just from you," she said.

His heart hammered against his rib cage. "This is a bad idea."

"There are worse ideas," she countered.

He felt himself begin to sweat. How could Laila's little sister affect him this way? It wasn't possible.

Dear Reader,

Have you ever felt invisible? Like you could jump up and down and scream and the person you're trying to reach *still* wouldn't see you? I have, and it's a terrible feeling. It could almost make you feel like you need to do something desperate to get that person's attention. That's part of what's happening to my heroine, Abby Cates. She has wanted to get the attention of the man of her dreams for what feels like forever. Now it looks as if she may finally get her chance.

In *A Maverick for Christmas,* we sled into the holiday season in Thunder Canyon with another couple ripe for romance. When Abby, "the invisible woman," does everything in her power to turn Cade Pritchett's head, he doesn't know what hit him, but he sure does like it. Can a lifelong crush really lead to true love?

Curl up and enjoy the ride! All the Thunder Canyon Mavericks and I are wishing you the warmest, most loving and joyous holiday season ever!

xo,

Leanne Banks

A MAVERICK
FOR CHRISTMAS

LEANNE BANKS

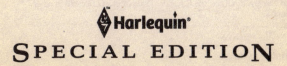

Harlequin®

SPECIAL EDITION

If you purchased this book without a cover you should be aware that this book is stolen property. It was reported as "unsold and destroyed" to the publisher, and neither the author nor the publisher has received any payment for this "stripped book."

Special thanks and acknowledgment to Leanne Banks for her contribution to the Montana Mavericks: The Texans are Coming! continuity.

Recycling programs for this product may not exist in your area.

ISBN-13: 978-0-373-65633-2

A MAVERICK FOR CHRISTMAS

Copyright © 2011 by Harlequin Books S.A.

All rights reserved. Except for use in any review, the reproduction or utilization of this work in whole or in part in any form by any electronic, mechanical or other means, now known or hereafter invented, including xerography, photocopying and recording, or in any information storage or retrieval system, is forbidden without the written permission of the publisher, Harlequin Enterprises Limited, 225 Duncan Mill Road, Don Mills, Ontario M3B 3K9, Canada.

This is a work of fiction. Names, characters, places and incidents are either the product of the author's imagination or are used fictitiously, and any resemblance to actual persons, living or dead, business establishments, events or locales is entirely coincidental.

This edition published by arrangement with Harlequin Books S.A.

For questions and comments about the quality of this book please contact us at Customer_eCare@Harlequin.ca.

® and TM are trademarks of Harlequin Books S.A., used under license. Trademarks indicated with ® are registered in the United States Patent and Trademark Office, the Canadian Trade Marks Office and in other countries.

www.Harlequin.com

Printed in U.S.A.

Books by Leanne Banks

LEANNE BANKS

is a *New York Times* and *USA TODAY* bestselling author who is surprised every time she realizes how many books she has written. Leanne loves chocolate, the beach and new adventures. To name a few, Leanne has ridden on an elephant, stood on an ostrich egg (no, it didn't break), gone parasailing and indoor skydiving. Leanne loves writing romance because she believes in the power and magic of love. She lives in Virginia with her family and four-and-a-half-pound Pomeranian named Bijou. Visit her website, www.leannebanks.com.

This book is dedicated to Susan Litman. You know why.

Prologue

Abby Cates remembered the moment she fell for Cade Pritchett. She had been nine years old at the time, and he'd been giving swimming lessons at Silver Stallion Lake. At seventeen, Cade had been tall, strong and blond. He was nice to all the kids, but demanded they learn their strokes. Abby was pretty sure he didn't remember scooping her out of some too-deep water when she'd choked and panicked. In her little-girl mind, Cade was a god.

Despite her best efforts, Abby had never found any man who could top Cade in her mind, not even now that she was twenty-two. And that was a terrible shame, especially since he'd never noticed her and, on top of that, wedding fever was running through Thunder Canyon like a bad flu.

Now that her older sister Laila was engaged to Jackson Traub, the discussions of weddings were nonstop. Her mother was usually so eager for Christmas that she began decorating plans in early November, but this year she was clearly distracted. If her mother didn't take a little break from wedding talk, then Abby was going to explode through the roof of her family's home. She tried not to listen to her mother's phone conversation as she finished cleaning up the kitchen after dinner.

"A double wedding for Marlon and Matt," her mother cooed. "Love is definitely in the air. And soon enough, there will be babies," she continued, her tone giddy with delight.

Abby glowered. *Love is in the air.* Yeah, for everyone except her. Her mother began to dig for more details on the double wedding of her cousins, and Abby turned the water on high as she washed the last pot. She wished she could wash out her brain as easily as she could clean the dishes.

Why in the world had she fallen for a man who couldn't seem to even notice her? Talk about unrequited love. Then it had gone from bad to worse when he'd dated her beautiful oldest sister, Laila, the town beauty queen. Then it went from worse to tragic when he'd proposed to Laila. At least her sister had turned him down, but she'd hated the idea that Cade would suffer from Laila's rejection.

The past couple of years it had been so hard to see Cade with Laila. Abby had felt as if she'd walked around with a permanent knot in her stomach. In love with her sister's on-again, off-again boyfriend? It was like a bad soap opera. Although she loved Laila, Abby had been torn between guilt and resentment. She'd successfully kept it hidden, but she didn't know how much longer she could manage it, especially since it felt as if everyone around her was finding love and getting married. And as far as Cade Pritchett was concerned, she might as well be invisible.

Irritated with her bad mood, she muttered to herself, "Suck it up. Wedding fever won't last forever, and Christmas is right around the corner."

One second later, the door opened and her sister Laila waltzed in wearing a smile and flashing a cover of a bridal magazine. "I guess I need to start planning for the big day."

Abby felt something inside her rip. The beginning, she feared, of turning into a rocket and shooting through the roof. If she didn't get out of here. "Gotta go," she said, tossing the towel she held on the counter. "I'll be back later."

Laila shot her a bemused look. "Where are you going?"

"I need to do some research for a paper," Abby manufactured, although it was partly true.

"Can't you do it online?" Laila asked.

"Nope. Tell Mom when she gets off the phone," Abby said and grabbed her coat. She jammed her hands through the sleeves and raced outside. Full of so many different emotions, she walked blindly away from the house. She skipped getting into her orange Volkswagen Beetle, hoping the cold air would freeze her feelings.

She was torn between swearing a blue streak and crying. She hated to cry, so she began to swear under her breath. Walking toward town, Abby whispered every bad word she could call to mind. At a younger age, she would have gotten her mouth washed out with soap, but there was no one to tattle on her unless she counted the bare November trees and whistling wind. Unfortunately she used up her repertoire very quickly, and despite her best efforts, her eyes filled with tears.

Chapter One

It had been a long day and it was colder than a well-digger's backside. Cade had been working like a dog and wanted a little reward. He wouldn't be getting it from a woman tonight, so Cade Pritchett looked inside the café, trying to decide whether or not to indulge in a slice of cherry pie.

Cade looked away. Since that insane moment he'd proposed to Thunder Canyon's beauty queen, the woman he'd dated casually the past few years, he'd become all too aware of his burning need for a family of his own. It didn't make sense because Cade wasn't interested in falling in love. He'd done that once and lost the woman to an accident. He wasn't interested in risking his heart, but he wanted more than what he had now. A partnership in his father's business, his own spread

just outside of town and his hobby rebuilding motorcycles. Oh, and his hound dog, Stella. He should have
listed her first.

From his side, he heard a sniffling sound. Curious,
he glanced over and saw Abby Cates wiping her nose
as she leaned against the café window. His stomach
clenched. Abby, little sister of the woman he'd asked to
marry him during the Frontier Days celebration. That
had been a monumental mistake.

He heard Abby sniff again and Cade felt a surge of
concern. He should check on the girl. The poor thing
looked upset. He moved toward her.

"Hey, what's up? Or down?"

Abby glanced up in shock, her wide eyes blinking
in surprise. "Hi," she said and gave another sniff and
surreptitious wipe of her nose with her tissue. "What
are you doing here?"

"Thinking about getting a piece of pie," he said.
"Long day."

She nodded and blinked away her tears. "This is the
beginning of one of your busy seasons, isn't it?"

"Yeah, how'd you remember?" he asked.

"Osmosis," she said. "I guess I eventually noticed
during the last few years when you didn't hang around
the house as much."

"Yeah," he said. "So, what's with the sniffles? I don't
think it's allergies or a cold."

She shrugged and lowered her gaze, her eyelids
hiding her emotions from him. "I don't know. Lots of
changes going on at my house. I guess I'm going to miss

Laila now that she's getting married," she said, then froze and met his gaze. "I'm so sorry. I didn't mean to say—"

He waved his hand in dismissal. "No problem. My pride was hurt more than anything else. Laila and I were never crazy in love. I shouldn't have been such a darned fool by proposing to her," he said.

"You weren't the fool. Laila was. She should have never let you get away," she said.

Cade laughed and shook his head. It felt nicer than he'd like to admit for Abby to rush to his defense, but he knew more than most that romance and emotion could be fickle and elusive. He shoved his hands into the pockets of his sheepskin jacket. "You shouldn't be out here in the cold," he said. "Let me buy you a cup of hot chocolate."

She met his gaze for a long moment, and he saw a flurry of emotions he couldn't quite name except one. Defiance.

She licked her lips. "I'd like something a little stronger than hot chocolate."

Surprise punched through him. "Something stronger," he said. "You're a little young for that, aren't you?"

She gave a husky chuckle. "Are you suffering from a little dementia due to your advanced years? I'm twenty-two."

"Whoa," he said. "When did I miss that?"

"I guess you weren't looking," she said wryly. Her chocolate-brown eyes flashed with humor, and his gaze slid over her silky, long brown hair.

"I guess not," he said. "So you want to go to the Hitching Post?"

"Sure," she said with a shrug, and they walked down the street to the town's most popular bar and hangout. It was crowded when they walked inside, so he hooked his hand under her elbow and guided her to the far end of the bar.

"Hey, Abby," a young man said from halfway across the room.

She glanced up and shot the guy a smile.

"Hi, Abby," a young woman called.

"Hey, Corinne," she said.

"You seem pretty popular here," Cade said, finding a space next to the bar. "How often do you come?"

She shook her head and rolled her eyes. "I know those people from my classes at college. I'm usually too busy to spend much time here. They're probably surprised to see me here."

He nodded. "What do you want to drink?"

"A beer's okay," she said with a shrug.

He noticed her lack of enthusiasm. "What kind?"

"Whatever you're having is fine," she said.

He felt a twinge of amusement. "You really don't like beer."

"I'm working on it," she said. "At least once a year."

He laughed out loud. "I'll get you one of those pink girly drinks. Cosmo," he said to the bartender. "And a beer for me. Whatever you have on draft."

Moments later, she sipped her pink martini and he drank his beer. "It's loud in here," he said.

She stirred her drink with the tiny straw. "Yeah, I guess that might bother you older folks," she said with a naughty smile.

He shook his head. Her teasing gave him a kick. "Yeah, I'm thirty. Don't rub it in. What have you been doing lately?"

"School. College," she corrected. "I'm also working at the youth center. And as you know, my family can get a little demanding. I have a part-time job teaching skiing lessons at the resort when I can fit it in. What about you? How's that new motorcycle coming?"

He was surprised she'd remembered. "Close to perfection, but I'm still tinkering with it."

"You wouldn't know perfection if it slapped you in the face," she teased.

Cade liked the way her long eyelashes dipped over her eyes flirtatiously. Someday, Abby could be trouble, he thought. "What do you mean by that?"

"I mean you have that perfection complex. Nothing you do is ever good enough. Not with your woodworking. Not with your motorcycle."

She nailed him in one fell swoop, taking him off guard. "How'd you know that?"

"I've known you for years." She took the last sip of her cosmo martini. "How could I not know that?"

For one sliver of a second, she looked at him as if he was a dork then shrugged. "You want another one?" he asked.

She shook her head and smiled. "No. I'm a light-weight. Already feel this one. I'll take some water."

Cade ordered water for her and continued talking with Laila's little sister with whom he'd played board games and computer games when he'd been waiting for Laila. He was distracted by her mouth. Especially when she licked her lips after taking a sip of her water. Her lips were plump, shiny and sexy. He shouldn't notice, but he sure did.

"So you're busy at work," she said and took another long sip of water. "Bet your father's driving you crazy."

"Yeah," he admitted. "No need to repeat that."

She laughed. "I won't. That could be tricky working with your dad. I mean, I love my own dad, but I can't control him."

"That's for sure," he said, thinking of his own father.

She clicked her half-empty water glass against his beer and dipped her head. "We agree. Cheers."

"So, what are you majoring in?" he asked.

"Psychology. I finish next spring, but I may need to get an advanced degree. I like working with the teens."

"I can see where you would be good at that," he said, thinking that although Abby appeared very young, she was pretty mature for her age.

"I don't know what I'll do after I graduate. I haven't decided if I'll leave Thunder Canyon or not," she said.

Her statement gave him a start. "You would leave town?"

"I may have to if I want to get an advanced degree. Plus, with everything going on with my family, it may be time for me to strike out on my own by then."

He nodded. "If you wanted to stay, you could get an

advanced degree online. And just because you move out of your parents' house doesn't mean you have to move out of town."

She smiled. "You almost sound like you'd like me stay. That can't be true. You barely notice me."

"You're a quality girl—" He broke off. "Woman," he corrected himself. "I hate to see Thunder Canyon lose a good woman like you."

"Ah, so it's your civic duty to encourage me to stay here," she said.

He felt a twist of discomfort. "Lots of people would miss you."

"Well, I haven't made any decisions yet. I need to finish my classes first. I'm just glad the end is in sight. What do you think about the rivalry between LipSmackin' Ribs and DJ's Rib Shack?"

Cade would have had to have been deaf and blind not to know about the controversy between Thunder Canyon's longtime favorite barbecue restaurant DJ's Rib Shack and the the new rib place, which featured waitresses dressed in tight T-shirts. "I'm a DJ's man all the way. I don't like it that the Hitching Post started featuring LipSmackin' Ribs on the menu and I refuse to order them. I'll buy drinks here, but no ribs."

"So you've never even visited LipSmackin' Ribs?"

"I went a few times just to see what the fuss was about," he said.

"You mean the skimpy uniforms the waitresses wear," she said.

He shook his head and rubbed his jaw. "I pity your

future boyfriend. He won't be able to pull anything over on you."

"Future? How do you know I don't have a boyfriend right now?" she asked. "I don't, but I certainly could. There are even some men who think I'm attractive, some who ask me to go out with them."

"I didn't mean it that way. And you be careful about those guys. You make sure they have the right intentions."

She shot him a playfully sly look so seductive he almost dropped his beer. "What would you say are the right intentions?" she asked.

His tongue stuck in the back of his throat for a few seconds. "I mean just that—you need to make sure they have the right intentions. You shouldn't let anyone take advantage of you."

"Unless that's what I want him to do, right?"

He choked on his beer. Where had this vixen come from? Although she'd been a spirited competitor whenever she'd played games and been far more knowledgeable about sports than most females he knew, Cade had always seen her as Laila's sweet little sister. "I think it's time for you to go home. I'm starting to hear things come out of your mouth that aren't possible." He waved for the bartender to bring the bill.

"Oh, don't tell me I scared big, strong Cade Pritchett," she teased as he finished his beer and tossed some bills on the counter.

"There's more than one way to scare a man. Let's go," he said and ushered her through the bar to the door.

* * *

Abby felt higher than a kite. She'd been waiting forever for the time when it was just her and Cade. She'd had a secret crush on Cade since even before her sister had dated him, and watching Laila's wishy-washy attitude toward Cade had nearly put her over the edge on more than one occasion during the past few years.

But now, she thought, her heart beating so fast she could hardly breathe, she had Cade all to herself, if only for a few more moments. "So is most of your work right now for people who want to get special Christmas gifts?"

"A good bit of it," he said. "But there's a potential for a big order. We'll find out soon." He stopped abruptly. "Is that old man Henson trying to change a tire on his truck?" he asked, pointing down the street.

Abby tore her gaze from Cade's and felt a twist of sympathy mixed with alarm. "I think it is. Isn't he almost eighty-five? He shouldn't be changing a tire during daylight let alone at this time of night," she said.

"Exactly," he said and quickened his pace. "Mr. Henson," he called. "Let me give you a hand with that."

Abby joined Cade as they reached the elderly man, who'd already jacked up the truck. "I'm fine," he said, glancing up at them, his craggy face wrinkled in a wince of pain. "It's these dang rusted bolts."

"Let me take a shot at them. Abby, maybe Mr. Henson might like a cup of that hot chocolate I was talking about earlier."

"I don't need any hot chocolate," Henson said. "I'm fine."

"I'm not," Abby said. "Would you keep me company while I drink some to warm me up?"

Henson opened his mouth to protest then sighed as he adjusted his hat. "Well, okay. But make it quick. I gotta deliver some wood in the morning."

Abby shot a quick look at Cade and shook her head. Mr. Henson was legendary for his work ethic. She admired him for it, but she also knew he'd gotten into a few situations where he'd had to be rescued. Flashing Henson a smile, she hooked her arm through his and walked to the café.

She made chitchat with the man while they sat in a booth and waited for their hot chocolate. She noticed Mr. Henson kept glancing out the window. "Your truck will be fine. It's in good hands with Cade."

"Oh, I know that," Mr. Henson said. "Cade's a fine young man. You'll do well with him."

She dropped her jaw at his suggestion then gave a wry laugh. "I think so, too, but I don't believe he sees me that way, if you know what I mean," she said and took a sip of the hot drink.

He wrinkled his already deeply furrowed forehead and wiggled his shaggy gray eyebrows. "What do you mean? You're a pretty girl. I'm sure you turn quite a few heads."

"Thank you very much," she said. "That means a lot coming from you."

"It's true. I've never been known for a silver tongue.

My Geraldine, rest her soul, would tell you the same. Although she *was* the prettiest woman to ever walk the streets of Thunder Canyon. I still miss her."

Abby slid her hand over Mr. Henson's. "I'm so sorry. How long were you married?"

"Fifty-three years," he said. "That's why I keep working. If I sit at home, I'll just pine. Better to be moving around, doing something."

"But you could afford to take a break every now and then. We don't want anything happening to you," she said and made a mental note to stop in and visit Mr. Henson. His loneliness tugged at her heart.

He shrugged. "I'll go when the good Lord says I'm ready, and not a minute before." He glanced outside the window. "Looks like Cade's finished changing my tire. We should go now. Let me pay the bill. And don't you argue with me," he said when she'd barely let out a sound. "I don't get to share some hot chocolate with a girl as pretty as you very often these days."

"And you said you didn't have a silver tongue," she said. "Thank you."

The two left the café and caught up with Cade, who appeared to be looking for a place to wipe some of the grease off his hands. Abby offered the paper napkin she'd wrapped around her cup of hot chocolate.

He made do with it. "Thanks," he said then glanced at the truck again. "It's no wonder you had trouble with those bolts. I had to bang on them to get them loose. You'll get that tire repaired soon, won't you?" he asked.

"I'll get to it. I'll get to it," Henson said in a testy

voice as he inspected the job Cade had done changing his tire. "Thank you," he said with a nod. "What do I owe you?"

Cade shook his head. "Nothing," he said.

"Aw, come on. I gotta give you something for your trouble," Henson said.

"Okay, I'll tell you what you can give me," Cade said. "You can stay out of trouble."

Henson glared at Cade for a moment then laughed. "I'll see what I can do. Thank you again. And, uh—" He glanced at Abby. "Take care of that pretty girl. You shouldn't let a good one like her get away."

Abby shot a quick look at Cade's disconcerted expression. Her face flamed with heat and she quickly focused her attention on her hot chocolate—blowing on it, sipping. "Thanks for the hot chocolate, Mr. Henson. Good night, now," she said.

She stood beside Cade as the old man got into the car and drove away.

"I'll give you a ride home. My car's just down the street. That Henson is a character, isn't he?" Cade muttered, leading her to his vehicle.

"I have to agree. So are you," she said, wishing the evening wouldn't end.

He opened the car door and glanced at her. "Me?"

"Yes, you," she said. "You're always trying to stay in the background, but here you go again saving the day."

"What do you mean?" he asked as he started the car.

"I mean you're always rescuing somebody. It's just what you do. White Knight syndrome?"

He looked at her for a long moment with an expression on his face that made her breath stop in her chest. He looked at her as if he were seeing her as more than Laila's little sister. "I didn't think anyone noticed," he finally said.

"Of course I notice," she managed in a voice that sounded breathless to her own ears.

He glanced away and put the car in gear, driving toward her home. Abby was torn between relief and disappointment. She had wanted that sliver of a moment to continue, yet she could breathe a little better now.

"Is that an official diagnosis? White Knight syndrome?" he asked, his mouth lifting in a half grin of amusement.

"No. I don't think you're clinically maladjusted. You're just a good man," she said, although *good* was putting it lightly. Cade was much more than a good man.

He glanced at her and chuckled. "Thank you. I feel better."

"That will be five dollars," she said and laughed at his sideways glance at her. "Just kidding. I'm not licensed to practice."

They approached her street and her stomach knotted. She tried to think of a way to continue this special time. She didn't want it to end. "I always thought that was strange. A doctor practices medicine. An attorney practices law. What if they have a lousy day practicing?"

Cade pulled the car to a slow stop and shifted into Park. "Good point. I try to avoid both if possible."

Abby drank in the sight of him, meeting his watchful blue gaze and noting the vapor of his breath from his mouth. His strong chin matched his character and determination and his broad shoulders had always made her think he could carry anything life threw at him. He'd suffered some deep losses. She knew that beneath that sheepskin jacket, his muscles were well developed from the times he'd played touch football with her extended family in the backyard.

She knew a lot about him, but she wanted to know so much more. She wanted to slide underneath that jacket and feel him against her. Maybe it was time to take a chance. A crazy chance. Her heart raced so fast she felt lightheaded.

"I've always liked your eyes," she said in a low voice.

His gaze widened in surprise. "What?"

"I've always liked your eyes," she repeated. "They say so much about you. You have this combination of strength and compassion and the first place you see it is in your eyes." She bit her lip then leaned closer to him. "Of course, the rest of you isn't bad, either."

"It's not?" he echoed. She saw a lot of curiosity and flickers of sensuality in his gaze.

"Not bad at all," she said, sliding her hand up the front of his jacket. Taking her courage in her hand, she tugged at his jacket to bring his head closer to hers. Then she pressed her mouth against his, relishing the sensation of his closeness and his lips meshed with hers. He rubbed his mouth against hers and she suddenly felt his hand at her back, drawing her breasts against his chest.

His response sent a flash of electricity throughout her and she opened her lips to deepen the kiss. He took advantage, sliding his tongue inside her. Craving more, she gave what she knew he was asking. Despite the cold temperature, she felt herself grow warmer with every passing second of his caress. Warm enough to strip off her coat and…

Cade suddenly pulled his mouth from hers and stared at her in shock. "What the—" He shook his head and swore, taking a giant step away from her. "I'm sorry." He swore again. "I shouldn't have done that."

"But you didn't start it," she said, her heart sinking at his response.

He held up his hands. "No, really. I shouldn't—" He cleared his throat. "You go on home, now. I'll watch from here."

"But, Cade—"

"Go inside, Abby," he said in a voice that brooked no argument.

Still tempted to argue, Abby had pushed her courage as far as it would go tonight. She swung away from him, hopped out of the car and slammed the door behind her. Striding home, she was caught between euphoria and despair. He had kissed her back and he sure seemed to like it. For those few seconds, he had treated her like a woman he desired. This time she hadn't imagined the way he tasted, the way his lips felt against hers, his hand at her back, urging her closer. This time, it had been real.

But then the man had apologized for kissing her. The knowledge made her want to scream in frustration. Was she back where she'd started? Was she back to being Laila's little sister?

Chapter Two

Cade would have mainlined his third cup of coffee after lunch if it had been possible. He hadn't slept well last night and had felt off all day. He stripped another screw for the designer desk he was making for an entertainment hotshot in L.A., and swore under his breath.

His father and partner, Hank, was talking, but Cade was trying to focus on the desk instead of the way Laila's sister had kissed him last night. And worse yet, he thought, closing his eyes in deep regret, the way he'd kissed her back.

Cade tried to shake off the thoughts and images that had been tormenting him since he'd apologized and burned rubber back to his house. Thoughts about her had haunted him. Her wide brown eyes, her silky, long brown hair and her ruby lips swollen from the friction of his mouth against hers. His own lips burned with the memory, and he rubbed the back of his hand against them, trying to rub away the visual and the guilt. What the hell had he been thinking?

Impatience rushed through him and he grabbed a file. His mind torn in different directions, he stabbed his other hand. Pain seared through him, blood gushed from his hand. Cade swore loudly and stood.

"What are you doing, son?" his father demanded, striding toward him to take a look at Cade's hand.

"It's fine," Cade said. "I'll bandage it and it will be fine."

"You better be up-to-date with your tetanus shot," Hank said.

"I am," Cade said. "I'm not that stupid."

"Based on your performance this morning…" his father began.

"Lay off, Dad," Cade said, looking down at the man who had taught him so much about carpentry and life, the man who'd never recovered from the death of his wife several years ago. None of them had really recovered from the death of Cade's mother. She'd balanced her husband's stern taskmaster nature with softness and smiles.

"Son, I don't want to have to say this, but you need to snap out of your funk. Laila is getting married to someone else, and you're just going to have to get used to it," Hank said bluntly.

Shock slapped through Cade as he stared at his father. He opened his mouth to say he hadn't been thinking about Laila then closed it. He sure as hell didn't want to tell his father he'd been thinking about Laila's little sister Abby.

"You bandage up that hand and go check in on the community center. They've requested a few things for their Thanksgiving program."

Cade shook his head. "We don't have time for me to go to the community center now. We have too much work."

Hank shook his head. "Get some air, do something different. You'll come back better than ever."

"You know that since we're equal partners, you can't be giving orders," Cade said.

Hank sighed and rolled his eyes. "Okay, consider it a request from your elderly father."

Cade felt a twitch of amusement. His father was still a hard driver, especially in the shop. "Elderly my—"

"Get on out of here," Hank said.

Cade pulled on his jacket and walked out the door, feeling his father's gaze on him as he left. He didn't want his father worrying about him. With a few exceptions during his teen years, Cade had made a point of not causing his parents much grief. Once his mother had gotten sick, his younger brothers had acted up, and Cade knew his father had needed to be able to rely on him. Work had gotten them through the rough times, and for Cade, the loss hadn't stopped with his mother. There's been Dominique and he'd felt the promise of happiness with her before she'd been taken from him.

Stepping outside the shop, he walked toward the

community center a few blocks away. He shook his head, willing the cold air to clear it. He shouldn't be thinking about Abby. It was wrong in so many ways. Putting his mind on the community center's Thanksgiving needs should point him in a different direction. He welcomed the change.

Cade walked inside the glass door of the community center and headed toward the gym at the back of the building. He pushed open the door and his breath hitched at the sight before him. The object of his distraction handed a baby to the community center's children's director, Mrs. Wrenn, and began to climb a ladder holding a humongous horn of plenty.

"What the hell?" he muttered, walking toward the front of the room.

Abby continued to climb the ladder while she lugged the horn of plenty upward. Cade couldn't permit her to continue. "Stop," he said, his voice vibrating against the walls.

Abby toppled at the sound of his voice and whipped her head in his direction. "Cade?"

"Stay right there," he said, closing the space between him and the ladder. He grabbed each side of the metal ladder. "Okay, you can come down now."

Abby's hair swinging over her shoulders, she frowned at him. "Why? I've just got a little farther to go."

"Not while I'm here," he said, his voice sounding rough to his own ears.

Abby shook her head. "But it won't take another minute for me to finish—"

"Come down," he said. "It's not safe. I'll handle it."

She paused long enough to make him uncomfortable. "Abby," he said.

"Okay, okay, but I was doing fine before you got here," she said, descending the ladder.

"That's a matter of opinion," he muttered under his breath as he watched her bottom sway as she wobbled.

She missed the last step and fell against him. He caught her tight and absently grabbed the horn of plenty, his heart pounding.

"Oops," she said after the fact.

Some part of him took note of the sensation of her breasts against his chest, her pelvis meshed against his as she slid downward. His brain scrambled, but he fought it.

"I really would have been fine," she insisted.

"Yeah," he said, unable to keep the disbelief from his voice. "I'll handle the rest of this."

"You're not being sexist, are you?" she demanded. "Because I really *can* do this."

Cade felt his heart rate rise again. "Not sexist," he said. "Just practical. I'm more athletic than you are."

"I don't know," she said. "I played soccer and—"

"I have more upper-body strength," he said, deciding to end the argument once and for all.

He felt Abby's admiring gaze over his broad shoulders. "I can't argue with that," she said.

He felt an odd thrill that he quickly dismissed. "I'll

go ahead and hang this horn of plenty," he said. "Do you mind holding the ladder?"

"Not at all," Abby said cheerfully.

Cade climbed the ladder and hung the horn of plenty. He descended to the floor. "My father told me you need a few things for your Thanksgiving show."

Mrs. Wrenn jiggled the toddler and Abby extended her arms to the small boy. "Come here, Quentin."

The toddler fell toward her and Abby laughed, catching him in her arms. "Hiya, sweetie," she said.

The mocha-colored child beamed and giggled as Abby cradled him, clearly feeling safe with her. Cade saw a flash of Abby, laughing, burgeoning with pregnancy and another baby on her hip. Her brown eyes were sexy with humor and womanly awareness.

Cade shook his head, snapping him out of his crazy visual. "How can I help you, Mrs. Wrenn?"

The elderly woman beamed at him. "Thank you so much for coming. We need a ship hull and a table for the pilgrim and Native American dinner. It doesn't have to be too special."

"We can take care of that," Cade said. "We'll get a donated table and dress it up."

"That would be wonderful," Mrs. Wrenn said.

"And I'll work out something with a ship's hull during the next week. How many people do you want on it?"

Mrs. Wrenn winced. "Twenty."

"Whoa," he said. "Good to know. We can take care of that."

Mrs. Wrenn gave a big sigh and clasped her hands together. "Thank you. I knew we could count on you, Cade. We want to give all of the children a chance to feel like stars."

Cade nodded, catching Abby's eye and feeling a flash of kinship with her. He was surrounded by people who either were or felt as if they needed to be stars, but he couldn't be less interested. If he read Abby's wry gaze correctly, then she felt the same way.

"I can do that," he said.

"I knew you could," Mrs. Wrenn said.

He glanced at Abby and the sexy look in her gaze took him off guard. He fastened his gaze on the graying Mrs. Wrenn. "Any particular colors you have in mind?"

The director shrugged. "Harvest colors."

He nodded. "I'll take that back to the shop. Anything else you need?"

"Nothing else I can think of," Mrs. Wrenn said and glanced at Abby. "Is there anything else that comes to mind? Abby has been nice enough to fill in since my volunteer helper Mrs. Jones had to have bunion surgery."

Abby glanced at the director, then looked at Cade. "Not a thing, but if you get lost, you can contact Mrs. Wrenn or me."

"I don't get lost," Cade said.

"That's a shame," Abby said under her breath, then lifted her shoulders. "Then if you need suggestions."

He shot her a sideways look. "Who does Quentin belong to?" he asked, unable to squelch his curiosity.

Abby's gaze turned serious. "His mother, Lisa, has passed her G.E.D. and has completed her L.P.N. She wants to get her R.N. She's just nineteen and one of my ROOTS girls. I told her I would step in as often as possible during her education. She's halfway through her R.N."

He felt a shot of admiration. "You're a good friend."

"She's a good mom. It's the least I can do."

Cade's respect for Abby grew. Big brown eyes, long brown hair, she was just Laila's little sister, but now she seemed like so much more. He glanced at the toddler and couldn't hold back a smile. "How are you babysitting with your courses?"

"Just call me Superwoman," she deadpanned. "Kinda like you're Superman."

He felt a crazy hitch in his chest and inhaled quickly. "I'm no Superman."

"Nobody else knows that," she said and shifted the baby on her hip.

His mind flashed. Body. Baby. Come-hither smile. Heaven help him.

Cade cleared his throat. "I'll get back to the shop."

"Thank you for coming, Cade," Mrs. Wrenn said in her squeaky voice.

"Let us know when you need a break," Abby offered, her eyes lowered to a sexy half-mast.

Cade felt a rush of arousal race through him. He

swore to himself and turned away. "See you ladies later," he said.

"Anytime," Abby said, and the sexy invitation sent his blood rushing to his groin. Cade swore again, but he suspected the fresh air might not cure his distraction.

Abby was surviving at home, but barely. Although she was happy her sister Laila had found true love and wanted to marry, it was hard to deal with the constant wedding plans. Plus, her cousins were headed down the aisle, too.

Enough was enough and it felt like pulling teeth to get Cade to look at her as if she was more than a fourth grader. Reality beckoned, however, and Abby was forced to join her family for a dinner with Jackson Traub and his sister, Rose. Jackson had managed what many other men had tried by winning over her sister Laila.

"To Laila and Jackson," her father toasted, lifting his glass. "May your love be bigger than your wills."

"Here, here," Abby's mother said.

"Yeah," Abby muttered under her breath and took a big gulp of sparkling wine.

Laila beamed and looked at Jackson. The love between them sizzled. Laila lifted her glass to Jackson and her eyelids lowered in an intimate gaze. "Who would have ever known?"

"Who?" Jackson echoed and clicked her glass against his.

Abby felt a sliver of envy that traveled deeper than her soul. What she wouldn't give to have Cade look at her that way. *Not in this lifetime,* she thought.

Thank goodness the Cateses understood their priorities. Food was near the top of the list. Soon enough, a platter of roasted chicken was passed her way, followed by mashed potatoes. After that, green beans and biscuits.

Abby took a small spoonful of each dish as it passed. Her mind was preoccupied with Cade. Her appetite was nearly nonexistent. The good news was that everyone's attention was focused on Laila and Jackson, so no one would notice the fact that she wasn't the least bit hungry.

Abby nodded and smiled and pushed her food around her plate then murmured an excuse to get her away from the table. She sought peace in her backyard. It was freezing, but that was no surprise. Abby enjoyed the freezing air that entered her lungs. Despite the fact that it was too cold for words, she was thrilled with the solemn quiet her father's ranch offered at moments like these.

She meandered past the porch and shoved her hands into her pockets.

Seconds later, she heard voices from the back porch.

"I know it's crazy, but Laila is my dream come true," Jackson Traub said. "I never expected it, and she took me by surprise."

"I'm so glad," Rose Traub said. "I was surprised, but

happy when it happened. I love that you never thought it would happen to you."

"Thanks," Jackson said, unable to conceal his amusement.

"Humility is the beginning of wisdom," Rose said.

Jackson swore. "You're tough."

"You taught me. I'm just not sure I'll ever find my true love. Maybe he doesn't exist. I feel like I've dated every man in Thunder Canyon."

Abby swallowed a sound of frustration that threatened to bubble from her throat. Rose had been out with a *lot* of Thunder Canyon men. She'd even gone out with Cade, and that hadn't set well with Abby, at all.

"You haven't dated every man. There's still old man Henson and his friends," Jackson joked.

Abby resisted the urge to laugh, but Rose didn't. Her warm chuckle drifted through the cold air. "Thanks for the encouragement. Mr. Henson is eighty-five if he's a day."

"Just kidding," Jackson said. "But the truth is you can find your true love. I did. Don't give up."

"I'm not sure I can count on that," she said.

"Give it a little longer," Jackson said. "You might be surprised."

Seconds later, silence fell over Abby as she stood outside the deck in the dark. She wasn't quite sure what she should take away from the cold night and the conversation she'd overheard.

Abby stared into the horizon, feeling the stars from the sky watching over her. She should leave, she thought, but she felt the stars tracking her. She wanted—no, needed—to feel the stars guiding her to her future. More than anything, she wished a lucky star was shining down on her. A star of love. If not love, then an antidote for love.

Fixing her gaze on the brightest star, she felt a ripple of realization shimmy down her spine. She's wanted Cade as long as she could remember. She'd pushed herself to flirt with him the other night. Abby felt as if her passion for Cade would never be returned. But she would never be sure if she didn't put herself out there.

Abby had never been much of a flirt, and she had no idea how to be a seductress, but maybe she needed to give it her best shot now. Maybe she needed to do everything she could to make Cade see her as a woman, a desirable woman who wanted him. At that moment, she made a promise to herself. No more shy little sister, hiding behind Laila. Abby needed to find her inner sexpot.

Abby cringed at the thought. Okay, maybe not *sexpot,* but *seductress* had an empowering ring to it…when it didn't make her snicker.

Two days later, Cade took a break from work at the shop and headed for the new bakery in town, the Mountain Bluebell Bakery. He was feeling deprived lately and figured giving in to his sweet tooth was the least of possible evils. Cherry pie or something better sounded great.

He exhaled and his breath sent out a foggy spritz.

Noticing a crowd ahead, he slowed as he approached. A news team was interviewing several different citizens of Thunder Canyon.

"So, do you think a down-home ribs meal is good enough to keep customers happy?" the newscaster asked. "Or do you think tight T-shirts and short shorts are necessary in today's market?"

"Nothing wrong with short shorts and tight T-shirts," a man from the crowd yelled.

"But is it necessary?" the newscaster asked.

"Well," the man said, "I guess not. But it sure doesn't hurt."

The crowd laughed.

Suddenly a microphone was put in Cade's face. "What about you? Do you think a tight T-shirt and short shorts are more important than a home-cooked meal?"

"No," he said without hesitation. "The food and service are great at DJ's. No need for tight T-shirts."

The reporter moved past him and Cade automatically searched the crowd. His gaze landed on Abby on the opposite side of the street. He wondered what she thought of all this. She'd seemed a bit skeptical of the skimpy outfits of LipSmackin' Ribs.

Her gaze met his, and he lifted his hand and gave her the hi sign. She nodded and moved toward him.

Cade noticed the way her long brown hair swung over her shoulders. Her cheeks were pink from the cold and her plump lips shiny and distracting. She had the kind of lips any man would want to kiss.

"Hi," she said as she approached him. "Can you believe this?"

He nodded at the crazy press. "Not really. Who would have thought a debate over ribs would bring national news to Thunder Canyon?"

"I'm with you," she said, glancing over her shoulder at the crowd behind her. "What are you doing out and about?"

"I'm taking a break and checking out the new bakery down the street. I hear they've got some good stuff," he said.

"Mind if join you?" she asked.

Something told him he should refuse, but he didn't give in to it. "What about school?"

"I don't have a class until tonight."

He frowned. "You take night classes? Why don't you stick to day?" he asked.

Her lips twitched. "Because not all of my classes are available during the day."

"Hmm."

"Are you going to buy me a chocolate tart or not?" she asked.

He blinked. "Yeah, I'll buy you a tart. Let's go."

He led the way to the bakery and they ordered their pastries and coffee.

Moments later, the two of them sat at a table with coffee, a chocolate tart and a slice of cherry pie à la mode. Like many of the shops around town, the bakery featured both Thanksgiving and Christmas decorations. The shop owners in Thunder Canyon weren't dummies. They would maximize the holiday season to get the most out of it. Cade, however, wasn't big on Christmas since his mother and Dominique had died years ago.

Abby took a spoonful of chocolate tart into her mouth and closed her eyes in satisfaction. "Now, that is good."

"Yeah," Cade said, fighting a surge of arousal as he took a bite of his cherry pie.

"No, really," she said, lifting a spoon toward Cade. "You should try this."

Cade glanced into her brown eyes then felt his gaze dip deeper to her cleavage. When had Abby Cates gotten cleavage?

Cade cleared his throat. "I'm game," he said and opened his mouth.

He felt her slide the spoon and decadent chocolate past his lips onto his tongue. His temperature rose. He swallowed.

"Good," he managed.

"Of course it is," she murmured.

Cade met her gaze and felt a wicked stirring throughout him. Something about Abby made him…hard.

She took a sip of coffee and looked at Cade from the rim of her coffee mug. "Coffee's not really my favorite," she said. "When it comes to hot drinks, I'd rather have hot chocolate or apple cider."

"I'll take coffee," Cade said.

"But what if you had a choice?" Abby asked. "What would you choose?"

"Coffee with cream and hazelnut," he said.

"Smells delicious," Abby said, closing her eyes and smiling.

"But do you want to drink it?" he asked.

"Not so much," she said. "But I would love to smell it."

He chuckled and she opened her eyes. "What's wrong with smelling?" she asked.

"Nothing," he said. "Nothing at all."

She got to the end of her tart and there was one bite left. "Bet you want it," she said, waving the spoon in front of his mouth.

The motion was incredibly seductive, and he found himself craving what she offered. Or maybe he was craving what he wanted. He couldn't quite tell what Abby was offering, but it was a big no-no. Or was it?

He clasped his hand over hers, the last bite of chocolate hanging between them.

"Take it," she urged.

Her voice was too sexy to ignore. He grabbed her hand and drew it to his mouth. Cade enveloped the chocolate with his mouth and swallowed it down. The motion was both carnivorous and sexual.

Abby's brown eyes widened in surprise.

"What did you expect?" he asked.

"I don't know," she said. "Something more…"

"Polite?" he asked.

Her eyes darkened. "Maybe. If so, I'm glad I was wrong."

His gut tightened. "You need to be careful. You're asking for trouble."

"Just from you," she said.

His heart hammered against his rib cage. "This is a bad idea."

"There are worse ideas," she countered.

He felt himself begin to sweat. How could Laila's little sister affect him this way? It wasn't possible.

"Go away, little girl," he said and pulled back.

"I'm not a little girl," she said.

"You're too young for me," he said.

"Says who?" she challenged.

Her defiance caught him by surprise. "Says anyone with any sanity."

Abby leaned toward him, her eyes full of everything he shouldn't be thinking. "Haven't you heard? Sanity's overrated."

"I don't know what game you're playing, Abby. But I'm not playing," he told her with finality.

Chapter Three

Abby's ego bruised *again,* she buried herself in her
schoolwork and decided to follow up on her intention
to visit Mr. Henson. She hadn't seen his old truck in
town during the past few days and decided he might
enjoy some leftover chicken and dumplings Abby and
her mother had made last night. She also brought along
a wreath to add a little holiday cheer to his home, hoping it might lift his spirits. She drove her orange VW
toward his place and slowed as she turned onto his dirt
driveway. The ground was too frozen to allow the dust
to kick up the way it would in the summer, she thought
as she pulled in front of the old white farmhouse.

Although Mr. Henson did far more than most folks
thought he should, Abby knew he'd finally given up on
ranching several years ago and leased his acreage to

a local rancher. The old blue truck with peeling paint was parked next to the house, which meant he should be home.

Abby picked up the container of food and got out of her car. She noticed the steps to his porch were still crusty with ice and wondered if he had any salt she could throw on them for him. Knocking on the door, she paused and listened, but there was no response. She knocked again and heard a faint reply.

"Mr. Henson, it's Abby Cates. Are you okay?"

She heard the sound of slow footsteps and moments later, the door finally opened. Abby was surprised at the sight of him. His face was grizzly with white stubble, his hair hadn't been combed and his clothes were rumpled.

"What are you doing here?" he demanded in a cranky voice.

"I came to see you and I brought some chicken and dumplings," she said.

His eyes lit with faint approval. "Oh, well, that's nice of you. Come on in," he said and hobbled inside. "Where's that Pritchett young man? Aren't you two married?"

"No," she said. "Cade Pritchett barely knows I'm alive."

Mr. Henson glanced over his shoulder. "That's his mistake, I'd say."

She noticed his grimace as he took a step and her alarm buttons started to go off. "Mr. Henson, you're limping. What's wrong?"

He waved his hand. "Oh, it's nothing. Couple logs fell on my leg when I was delivering wood. You mind if I heat up those dumplings? I bet they're tasty."

"They are, but I think you might need to get your ankle checked by a doctor," she said.

"Doctors usually can't do anything. Medicine is just one more racket, I say."

"But—"

"You gonna make me beg for those dumplings?" he asked.

She sighed. "No. Sit down and I'll heat them up for you," she said and walked toward the kitchen, then turned as something occurred to her. "If you'll let me take you into town to see the doctor as soon as you finish eating."

He scowled at her. "I'm telling you, it's a waste of time and money."

"It will make me feel better," she told him. "I'm worried about you. You're not yourself."

His gaze softened. "Well, you're being silly," he said gruffly. "I'll go," he said, sinking onto the sofa. "But not until I eat those dumplings."

Thirty minutes later, he'd finished the food and she hung the wreath on his front door.

"What's that for?" he asked as he shuffled toward her car.

Abby adjusted the red bow. "To give you some Christmas spirit."

He muttered and got into her car. Abby drove toward

town with Mr. Henson fussing the entire way about her car.

"What can you carry with this thing, anyway? Bet my lawn-mower engine is bigger than this. What keeps it running?" he asked. "Sounds like squirrels."

"The only thing I have to carry is me," she said. "I don't haul wood, and this car is surprisingly good in the snow."

"Can't believe that," he said. "You'd get stuck in six inches."

"It's light, so it doesn't sink, plus the gas mileage is terrific. What kind of gas mileage does your truck get?"

He made a mumbling sound that she couldn't understand. "Excuse me? What did you say?"

"Fifteen miles to the gallon," he said. "But I could haul most of the houses around here if I wanted."

She bit her tongue, refusing to point out the obvious, that there was no need to haul houses. Turning off the main drive, she pulled next to the clinic door.

"This is a no-parking zone," he told her.

"I know," she said. "I just wanted to get you as close to the door as possible."

"Hmmph," he said and opened the car door.

"Just a minute," she said, cutting the engine and rushing to the passenger side of the car.

"Gotta be a darned pretzel to ride in that car," he grumbled, but leaned against her as she helped him inside the clinic. Two hours later, she helped Mr. Henson back to the car as he hobbled on crutches.

"Just a sprain," he said. "I told you it wasn't anything

and I'm not taking that pain medication. It makes me loopy."

"It's not a narcotic," she said as she carefully arranged the crutches in her backseat. "Do you have plastic bags?"

"Yeah, why?" he asked.

"For the ice. The doctor said you need to put ice on your ankle."

Mr. Henson shrugged.

"Well, if you don't want to get better and you want to keep feeling rotten, you don't need to follow his instructions."

She felt the old man whip his head toward her. "I didn't say that," he said.

"The doctor said between the bad bruise and sprain it's a wonder you didn't break it. So you need to take care of it. RICE is what he said."

"Yeah, yeah," he said. "Rest, ice, compression and elevation."

"You can sit back and watch some TV," she suggested.

"Hate that reality stuff. Give me a book or a ball game instead."

"That could be arranged," she said. "I think my mother said something about fixing some beef stew. Maybe I could bring some over for you if you behave yourself."

The old man licked his lips. "That sounds good."

She smiled. "You'll get better faster if you do what the doctor says."

"Maybe," Mr. Henson said and paused. "You know, you would make a good wife. You nag like a good wife would."

Abby didn't know whether to feel complimented or insulted.

"Cade Pritchett will be chasing you sooner than you think," he said.

"Not in this lifetime," she said.

Mr. Henson lifted a wiry gray eyebrow. "You disrespecting your elder?"

"No," Abby said reluctantly. "I just can't fight reality."

"Girlie," he said, "I'm eighty-five and I lost Geraldine, my reason for living, eight years ago. I fight reality every day."

She couldn't argue with that.

After that, Abby focused on her schoolwork and her work at ROOTS, a community group founded for at-risk teens. Abby led her girls' teen group on Tuesday nights where they talked about everything from bullies and sex to cosmetics and higher education.

The truth was most of the girls in Abby's group were pretty cool. They were older than their years and saw Abby as the person they wanted to become. She was humbled by their admiration.

"So, we've told you about our guys. When are you gonna tell us about yours?" Keisha, a wise-to-the-world fifteen-year-old, asked.

"I don't really have a guy," Abby said.

Silence settled over the group and Abby felt an unexpected spurt of discomfort. "Well, I *could* have a guy. It's just that the guy I want doesn't see me."

Shannon, a sixteen-year-old with purple hair, frowned. "Is he blind?"

Abby chuckled. "Not in the physical sense. He used to date my sister, so he sees me as the little sister."

"Oooh," Katrina, who wore faux black leather from head to toe, said. "Drama. I love it. Does your sis know you like the guy?"

Abby shook her head.

"Does *she* like this guy?" Keisha asked.

"Oh, no. She's engaged to someone else."

"Well, then, you should definitely move in on him," Katrina said.

Abby laughed uncomfortably. "He sees me as the little sister."

"You should change that," Shannon said. "Maybe you could dye your hair pink."

"I'm not sure that's me," Abby said.

"Well, you have to do something different," Shannon said, her gaze falling over Abby in a combination of pity and disapproval. "You're, like, everything but sexy."

"She's not ugly," Keisha said.

"I didn't say that," Shannon said. "She's just not sexy."

"I don't know," Katrina said. "She's got that fresh, natural, girl-next-door look."

"But *not* sexy," Shannon repeated.

Silence followed.

"We could help you," Shannon said.

Alarm slammed through her. "Help?" she echoed in a voice that sounded high-pitched to her own ears.

"Yeah," Keisha said, clearly warming to the idea. "We can sex you up. Your guy won't be able to ignore you then."

"I'm not sure…" Abby said.

"Hey, it's like you always tells us," Shannon said. "If you always do what you've always done, you'll always get what you've always gotten."

Abby blinked at the sound of her words played back to her. True, but how much of a change was she willing to make?

"If you won't do pink or blond hair, then we can do big hair," Shannon said, pursing her profoundly pink lips.

"And cat eyes," Keisha added.

"And a short, black leather skirt," Katrina added.

Abby winced inwardly. *Black leather skirt?*

Shannon nodded. "Kim Kardashian hair. He won't know what hit him."

Abby managed to redirect the conversation, but she knew her girls were determined to perform a drastic makeover. She ran into her fellow ROOTS volunteer, Austin Anderson, after the meeting. Austin was twenty-four years old and the two of them were good friends, thanks to their time spent working together.

"How's it going?" Austin asked and stepped beside

her as she walked toward her car in the small parking lot.

"Okay," she said and knew her voice didn't hold the commitment it should have.

Austin laughed. "Let's try this again," he said. "How's it going?"

"I think I may have just gotten myself into a situation," she said as she drew close to her car.

"What kind of situation?" he asked, putting his hand against her car door before she could open it.

Abby sighed and turned to lean against the car. She reluctantly met his gaze. "I did a bad thing," she said.

"You sold drugs or killed a baby," he said.

She couldn't withhold a chuckle. "Neither. I did, however, get drawn into a discussion about my personal life with my ROOTS girls group. Now they want to perform a sexy makeover."

He laughed. "Hooker time."

She shot him a sideways glance. "Kinda. But they make an important point. They repeated my words of wisdom back to me. If you always do what you've always done, you'll always get what you've always gotten."

He nodded. "Okay."

"Well, if I go through with this makeover, I may need a cohort."

Austin stared at her for a long moment. "I'm not sure this is a good idea."

"It probably isn't, but I need to shake things up."

Austin gave a heavy sigh. "What do you have in mind?"

"I dress up in makeover mode. You and I hit the town in places where people will talk. My unrequited love wakes up and sees that I am the answer to his heart's desire."

Austin winced. "Abby, I'm really not sure this is a great idea."

"I'm sure it isn't," she said. "But I have to do something to shake up Cade's impression of me."

"Cade?" Austin echoed. "Cade Pritchett." He gave a low whistle and shook his head. "Isn't he the one who proposed to your—"

"Yes," she said in a flat tone.

Austin took a deep breath. "Okay, I'm in. Let me know when you want to do this."

"Apparently Saturday night," she said in a wry tone. "It's the most visible night."

Austin nodded and raked his hand through his hair. "All right. Text me with the time." Austin brushed his finger over her nose sympathetically. "You're a great girl. If he doesn't realize it, he's an idiot."

"So far, he's an idiot," she whispered, her heart hurting.

The following Saturday, the ROOTS teens performed their magic on Abby. As she stared into the mirror, she wasn't sure if it was magic or something more gruesome.

"Are you sure…" she began as she looked at her dark eye makeup.

"It's perfect," Keisha said.

"You are so hot," Katrina said. "You're going to knock every guy off his feet."

Abby was not at all sure. She squinted her eyes at her teased hair, trying to see a remnant of her usual self.

"Ready to go?" Austin asked from the back of the room.

Abby took a deep breath and turned to look at him.

"Oh. Wow," he said.

Abby felt a sudden spurt of panic. "What does *'Oh. Wow'* mean?"

Austin strolled toward her. "You look hot. You'll turn heads. Look out, Thunder Canyon."

Abby rose and walked toward him. "You're lying like a dog, aren't you?"

"Not at all," he said. "You're going to turn heads like nobody's business tonight. Are you ready?"

She met his gaze and quieted her crazy heartbeat. "Not really," she said. "But that first jump in cold water is the hardest. It may as well be now."

Abby and Austin visited the hottest bars and made sure she was seen by the maximum number of people. Their last stop was an old bar on Main Street. Surprisingly enough, Cade was at this bar watching a ball game. He didn't even notice her as she sashayed inside with Austin.

Austin, however, noticed Cade. He ordered Abby

another soda water, her fifth of the evening. She countered with a martini.

Austin raised his eyes. "Lemon drop?" he asked. "I'd say you've earned it."

Abby propped on a bar stool and tried to look flirty as she sipped her lemon-drop martini.

It was a little bitter, so she switched off to ice water. She jiggled her leg from the bar stool and wondered if Cade would ever tear his gaze from the screen.

Suddenly, Austin gave a loud laugh that startled her and vibrated throughout the bar. He leaned toward her and nuzzled her.

Abby blinked in shock. *Holy buckets.*

"Play along," he said in a low voice.

Oh, yeah, she thought and nuzzled him back and giggled. That was what she was supposed to do. Right?

Out of the corner of her eye, she saw Cade looking at Austin and her. He didn't look happy. She forced a light laugh.

"He's looking, isn't he?" Austin said as he lifted his fingers to her cheek.

"Yes," she said in a low voice.

"It's what you wanted, isn't it?" he asked.

Abby felt torn. "I guess."

Austin shook his head. "Better make up your mind. He's right behind you," he muttered. "Cade," he said. "Old man, how ya doing? I see a friend on the other side of the room. I'll be back in a minute—darlin'," he added to Abby.

Abby turned to look at Cade. His face looked like a thundercloud. "Hi," she said. "How's the game?"

He shrugged. "It's California against Clemson."

She smiled. "Not close enough to care."

"I guess. What the hell have you done to your hair?"

Abby frowned. "Dressed it up. Dressed me up," she said.

"You don't need to dress up," he said. "You're asking for trouble dressed like that."

Abby frowned at him, feeling a double spurt of frustration and anger. "Some people might say I looked pretty."

"Some people would say anything to get you into bed," Cade said.

Offended, Abby narrowed her eyes at him. "You just need to butt out of my date. I'm having a good time. There's nothing wrong with that."

Austin appeared from behind Cade and lifted his eyebrows. "Ready to go, sweetheart?"

Abby frowned in Cade's direction. "Sounds good to me," she said and rose from her bar stool. It took every bit of her concentration not to look at Cade. "G'night," she said, without meeting his gaze, and hooked her arm with Austin's as she strutted out of the bar.

As she and Austin stepped into the cold night, she sucked in a clean breath of air. "I'm not sure that worked."

Austin chuckled. "Well, I think you showed him what he's missing."

His sense of humor lifted her spirits. "Thanks for being a good soldier."

"It wasn't so bad. It's not like I have anyone waiting for me," he said.

She studied his eyes, trying to read him. "I would almost think there was someone you want waiting for you."

"Don't worry about it," Austin said, opening the passenger door to his SUV.

"Hmm," she said, wondering if Austin could have a crush on someone. And for whom would he be pining?

Austin drove her home and she stepped outside the car. "Thank you for indulging my craziness," she said.

Austin shrugged. "We're all crazy in our own special way."

Abby laughed. "Thanks. You make me feel a little better. I think you may have been right from the beginning. This wasn't a great idea."

"You never know," he said. "He might surprise you."

"I won't count on it," she said. "But thanks, anyway."

She watched as he pulled out of her driveway then reluctantly turned toward her home, wondering if she could make it to her bedroom before any of her family saw her because they would give her a hard time for dressing so out of character. The house wasn't well lit. Abby suddenly recalled her mother mentioning something about a Brunswick-stew dinner being held at the local Knights of Columbus. Her father loved Brunswick stew and, if the dinners were cheap, she suspected the rest of her family was chowing down, too. Her mother must have been thrilled to skip meal preparation tonight.

She stomped through the frozen snow to the front door of her home and opened the door. She waited in silence, listening for signs of her family. Nothing. Thank goodness. She breathed a sigh of relief then suddenly heard a tap at the door.

Wincing, Abby eyed the peephole and got the shock of her life. She blinked to make sure she wasn't dreaming. It was Cade.

Taking a deep gulp of breath, she swung open the door. "Forget something?" she asked.

He narrowed his eyes at her. "You okay?"

"Of course I'm okay," she said, unable to conceal her impatience and a bit of witchiness.

His gaze fell over her. "I was worried about you," he muttered.

"Why?" she asked, leaning against the doorjamb.

"The way you were dressed. I didn't want your date to take advantage of you," he said.

"He was a perfect gentleman," Abby said.

"Yeah, well—" He sighed, his gaze falling over her. "You gonna invite me in?"

Surprised, Abby stepped backward. "Sure. Come on in."

The foyer was dimly lit by a lamp.

Cade stepped toward her and lifted his hand to her hair. "You don't need all this makeup and gunk clouding your natural beauty. What were you thinking?"

Abby swallowed over a lump of emotion. "Natural beauty?" she echoed.

"Yeah," he said and stroked her hair. "Why would you mess with this?"

She opened her mouth and stared at him. "Umm." She shrugged her shoulders. "I don't—"

His mouth descended onto hers.

Abby gasped, trying to swallow her shock.

"You're hot without all the makeup," he told her, and she felt her world turn upside down.

Somehow, the two of them stumbled to the couch in the den. She fell backward and he followed her down. His weight was the sexiest thing she'd ever felt in her life. She closed her arms and legs around him.

Cade devoured her mouth and slid between her legs. His hardness meshed against her, making her wish the clothes between them would dissolve. She wanted him inside her. There was no such thing as close enough.

He rubbed and she arched. His tongue tangled with hers. *Give me more,* she thought. *Give me all of you.*

Cade swore under his breath, but continued to kiss her. He kissed her as if she was the most important thing in the world. Abby was hot with want and need. She'd wanted him so long, so very long.

His hand slid to her breast and she stopped breathing. He rubbed her nipple. Abby arched toward him. He groaned into her mouth. The sound was so sexy she couldn't stand it.

"I want you so much," she whispered desperately.

"I want you," he muttered and thrust against her.

Abby heard, felt something in the room, but Cade overpowered her senses.

The sound of a gasp took her slightly away from Cade's spell. "What?" she murmured.

"Oh, my God. How perfect is this."

Abby blinked, hearing her sister's voice. She tugged her mouth from Cade's and felt him look in the same direction.

Laila smirked. "This really is perfect. Why didn't I see it before?"

Mere breaths later, he rose from Abby and stood. He glanced from Laila to Abby, but his gaze lingered on Abby. "Crazy," he said. "This was crazy. I can't explain it. I'm sorry. I should go," he said and left.

Abby stared after him, trying to compute everything that had happened. Why had he kissed her? She wondered what would have happened if Laila hadn't interrupted them. Abby felt a rush of frustration and met her sister's gaze.

"Oops," Laila said. "It could have been worse. Everyone else is on their way back from the Brunswick-stew dinner."

Abby rose from the couch. "Why don't I feel better?"

"It's not my fault I walked in on the two of you. It's not like you sent up a warning flare," Laila said.

Abby could have screamed. "Do you have any idea what it's like being your sister?"

Laila blinked. She winced. "That bad?"

"Beauty queen a gajillion times over, super successful. Worse, there's Cade."

Laila bit her lip. "How long…"

Abby shook her head. "Longer than you want to know."

Laila gave a slow nod. "Sorry," she said.

"Yeah," Abby said and rose from the couch.

"I gotta ask. What's with the outfit?" Laila asked, waving her hand toward Abby's leather skirt and tight top.

"It was an experiment," Abby said, not wanting to linger on her so-called makeover.

Laila laughed. "Bet you knocked Cade on his ass."

Abby bit her lip because she wasn't sure what Cade would do tomorrow. "I'd appreciate it if you wouldn't broadcast what you interrupted tonight," Abby said. "G'night."

Cade drove his SUV to his place outside of town. He was torn between arousal and the overwhelming feeling of insanity. What had he been thinking?

He had not been thinking. That was the point.

He'd seen Abby dressed like sex on a stick, felt protective and chased after her, then gave in to some insane urges. He was still hard from kissing and holding her. He had definitely gone insane and he needed to bring himself back to sanity, no matter how painful it was.

Pulling into his long driveway, he sucked in a deep breath and pulled to a stop. He cut the lights of his SUV and felt a sense of loneliness at the thought of nothing going on inside his house with no one waiting for him.

A sliver of Dominique slid through his mind like a

ghost. He remembered her black hair and her laughing black eyes. He'd hoped she could heal him, but he hadn't been sure. When he'd finally gotten around to deciding to ask her to marry him, she'd died in an automobile accident. That seemed as if it had been a lifetime ago. Years earlier, his mother had died and his family was trying to dig their way out of their grief.

After Dominique he'd just closed the door on his emotions. It had been the easiest route. Then, Laila had seemed just like him. Emotionally closed off. After dating her off and on for years, it had made sense to Cade for them to marry. In many ways, they were the same. They were getting to the place where they should go ahead and do the baby thing, so perhaps he and Laila should get married.

In retrospect, it had been a crazy idea, and he deeply regretted pursuing the possibility. Cade wanted a family of his own, and he hated that he wanted it. Life would be so much easier without that strong desire. He could work at his family's furniture shop, build his motorcycles, contribute to the community, take a woman friend every now and then and his life would be fine.

Right?

Or not.

Cade swore under his breath and raked his hand through his hair. He'd just made out with Laila's little sister. How screwed up could this situation be? Shaking his head at himself, he stepped out of his truck and walked into his lonely-ass house. The dog greeted him at the door. Thank goodness for man's best friend.

Strolling to the refrigerator, he grabbed a beer. The sound of his footsteps echoed on the wood floor of his foyer and kitchen. Is that what he was going to hear for the rest of his life? The sound of his boot heels on his own kitchen floor?

What was wrong with that?

He took a long swig of his beer and headed for the den, his dog, Stella, trailing after him all the way. Cade found the remote and turned on his giant flat-screen TV. He flicked through a few channels. Thank goodness there was a college football game. He didn't care who was playing.

Sinking down on his leather couch, he took another long swig of beer then sucked in a deep breath. He stared at the big-screen TV and waited for the game to anesthetize him. The thought of Abby's lips against his slid through is mind. The sensation of her lips, soft, silky, swollen, slick.

Her breasts had felt so good against his chest. Her nipples against his chest, his palm. Lower, lower, he'd rubbed against her. She'd arched against him.

He'd given in to the urge to slide his hands lower, to seek out her secrets. He'd felt her damp arousal.

Then Laila had walked in.

Cade swore under his breath. He didn't want to think about this anymore. He should focus on the game and his beer instead.

An hour and a half later, he woke himself up with a snort. He blinked, staring at the screen. The game was over. An infomercial about an exercise machine was playing.

Cade stared at it for a few minutes then flicked off the TV. A soft lamp kept the darkness from completely enveloping him. In the past, the darkness had been comforting. But now...

Now he wanted more and now he wanted Abby. And that was insane. Super insane.

His body grew hard too quickly and he swore again. Rising from the couch, he headed for the shower. Cade turned the water on cool, stripped off his clothes and stepped inside. A hot shower would have felt a lot better, but he needed to get away from his need for Abby. A cold shower should cure him. That was all he needed to knock some sense into himself and Abby out of his mind.

Chapter Four

Cade did what he'd always done when he was bothered about something. He threw himself into his work. It was good timing because between the approach of the holidays and some new high-dollar custom orders, Pritchett & Sons were slammed.

He sanded a bed head in preparation for stain. A man had commissioned this piece for his wife for their tenth anniversary. It would be a nice piece when he finished it, Cade thought, feeling a nip of envy over the customer's good luck of having a woman and children in his life.

Narrowing his eyes, he refocused on the work at hand. A family just wasn't in the cards for him. At least, not now. Cade heard his brother using the electric screwdriver on a table he was making and glanced over at him. Dean was good company because he didn't talk all that much. Cade couldn't have abided much chattiness at the moment. He was too busy trying to quiet his own mind.

Dean met his gaze and nodded in the direction of the bed head. "That's looking good."

"Yeah, I think Mr. Winston will be pleased with it. Hopefully Mrs. Winson will, too," he said wryly. He'd learned through the years that women often didn't see things the same way men did.

Dean nodded and gave a low chuckle then got back to work.

Cade continued sanding. He found the rhythm of woodworking both soothing and absorbing. From an early age, when his father had taught him the basics, Cade had envisioned little touches he'd wanted to add in the pieces on which he'd worked. His father hadn't discouraged him, and although Hank was more focused on producing solid, basic furniture, Cade had taken an artistic bent.

Within the past few years, people had sought him out for his one-of-a-kind pieces, even asking for his signature on the finished furniture. At first, it had seemed silly to Cade, but the request for his signature had become so frequent, it was now almost a routine.

Nearly finished with the sanding, Cade heard the shop door open and glanced up to see their regular courier, Mike Jones, loaded down with boxes. "Hey, Mike, let me give you a hand with that," Cade said, rising from his bench.

"Thanks. I've got more in the truck."

"I can help," Dean said.

Cade took the boxes into the back room to sort them out later. Seconds later, Dean and Mike brought in more. "You can tell it's the holiday season just by the number of packages," Cade said.

"For darn sure," Mike said, pulling out his electronic gizmo for Cade's signature. "Unfortunately, holidays can bring out the wackiness in people." He shook his head. "I just made a delivery to the Tattered Saddle and Jasper demanded that I wait while he opened the packages. He tore through them and apparently didn't find what he was looking for. I was waiting for his signature, and he called somebody on the phone yelling about some missing package. And then, I must not have heard correctly, but the old man said something about how the Rib Shack may not be as easy to take down as expected."

Clearly rattled, Mike shook his head again. "Gotta run. More deliveries. See you guys later and thanks for being *sane*."

The courier ran out the door, leaving a rush of cold air in his wake. Cade looked at Dean and saw the same mixture of alarm and confusion written on his brother's face that he felt. "What the—"

Dean lifted his shoulders in confusion. "I've always thought Jasper was odd, but I can't believe he's behind the problems at the Rib Shack. What would he have to gain?"

"You got me," Cade said. "Maybe it's like Mike

said and he didn't hear the old man right. Jasper's been known to mutter and mumble."

"Hmm," Dean said, the sound short and full of suspicion.

Cade shrugged it off. "We need to get back to work."

"Yeah. Same for me if I want to make that poker game tonight," Dean said, heading back to the table.

"Just be careful who you're playing with," Cade said.

"I know better than getting in a game with a bad crowd," Dean said with a scowl.

"Just a reminder from someone who's bailed you out a couple of times," Cade said.

"Three years ago," Dean said.

"Some things you don't forget. Like being woken up at 3:00 a.m. because your younger brother has been left in the snow wearing only a pair of underwear and his socks because he bet more than he had."

"Three years ago," Dean repeated with a sigh. "Thanks for coming."

"There was never a doubt I would do anything else."

Dean nodded and they returned to work, but Cade felt his mind turning to thoughts of Abby. He didn't like surprises and he was damn surprised that he'd acted like he had with her. He'd always viewed her almost as a little sister or cousin. She was his little buddy, he'd thought. Not a woman with whom he wanted to share a bed. Now she was someone who made him feel so worked up and *hot*.

Irritated with his distracting thoughts, he tossed his brush aside and stomped to the back room to get a cup of coffee. It may as well have been tar since he'd made it this morning. Sipping it, Cade grimaced and walked out the back door of the shop, hoping the cold air would clear his head and cool his body. A couple minutes later, he walked back inside and returned to his bench.

"You okay?" Dean asked.

"Yeah," Cade said, taking another sip of terrible coffee.

"There's a lot of talk about Laila and Jackson getting married. It's enough to get on anyone's nerves, let alone—"

Cade swore under his breath. "I'm okay with Laila marrying Jackson. I wish them well. Laila isn't who's bothering me."

Dean's eyebrows rose in surprise. "Then who is?"

Reluctant to discuss the subject with anyone, Cade shrugged. "Nobody is. It's just work. I have a lot of work to do. So do you."

"Yeah, whatever," Dean said. "You aren't usually this much of a pain in the butt to deal with just because you've got a lot of work to do."

Cade sighed at his brother's words. He'd been trying so hard not to think about Abby that he hadn't realized he'd been hard on everyone else. "It's not Laila. It's Abby."

"Abby?" Dean echoed. "Abby who? The only Abby I know of is Laila's little sister." Dean must have seen the conflicted expression on Cade's face. "Really? Abby Cates?"

"I'm not sure how it happened. I saw her crying a

few weeks ago and offered to buy her a hot chocolate. Somehow we ended up at the Hitching Post instead. I drove her home, and she kissed me."

"Whoa, that must have caught you off guard," Dean said. "It's always awkward when you have to tell a woman you're not interested." Silence followed. "You did let her know you weren't interested, didn't you?"

"Yeah, but then I saw her out with some guy, and she was dressed for trouble. I was worried about her, so I followed her home and we stopped talking and started—" He broke off. "Anyway, it's crazy. Abby's not my type. I can't see myself in a long-term relationship with her."

"Hmm," Dean said. "You don't think she's some kind of rebound fling for you, do you?"

"No," he snapped. "I wouldn't do that kind of thing to Abby. She's too good to be treated that way. And besides, I'm over Laila. I was never in love with her."

Dean lifted his hands. "Okay, okay. I'm on your side. Remember?"

Cade frowned. "Yeah, I know. I'm gonna take a walk. I'll be back in awhile."

In a town as small as Thunder Canyon, Abby was sure she'd run into Cade sooner or later, but it was as if he'd vanished. She knew he was putting in long hours at the shop, but still, she would have expected to see him out and about at one time or another. During the past week, she'd completed two papers, babysat for one of her ROOTS girls and endured hours of wedding-planning discussions from her mother and Laila. The good news was that her mother had started to set out snowmen and Santa figures inside the house. Abby could only hope the holidays would provide at least a slight reprieve from wedding talk.

Since she had walked in on Abby and Cade, Laila had tried to overcompensate by constantly remarking on how pretty and smart Abby was. Although Abby appreciated the sentiment, she wasn't interested in the extra attention. She really didn't want the rest of her family knowing about her unanswered quest for Cade. It was bad enough that Laila knew.

One of Abby's friends, Rachel, invited Abby to join her at the Hitching Post for a girls' night out. Ready for a break, she accepted. Although she didn't tease her hair like the girls at ROOTS had done, she realized she wanted to look more like a woman than a high-school girl, so she put on some mascara and lip gloss, changed into a sexy shirt and wore some high-heeled boots with her jeans. She looked in the mirror and shrugged at her reflection. No one would accuse her of being a beauty queen, but she supposed she looked a little better than usual.

"Abby," her mother called from the kitchen. "Rachel's here."

Grabbing her jacket, she headed for the front door where Rachel stood. Her father was sitting on the couch reading his paper. "Don't get into any trouble," he said.

Abby planted a kiss on his cheek and laughed. "Now, when have I ever caused you any trouble?"

"Hmmph," he said. "It's not too late. You be careful."

"You, too, Daddy. Too much bad news is bad for your health," she shot back with a cheeky grin. "Let's go," she said to Rachel and the two of them ran down the front steps to Rachel's six-year-old Ford Explorer. "Thanks for inviting me out," Abby said. "I need a break from everything," she said.

Rachel nodded. "Me, too. I turned in a ten-page paper this week."

"Multiply that times two," Abby said.

"At least you're getting near the end," Rachel said. "I'll have to take some courses in summer school to wrap everything up."

Abby knew Rachel and her boyfriend had recently decided to take a break and Rachel was very upset about it. "Heard anything from Rob lately?"

Rachel frowned. "Just some texts and Facebook messages."

"You could 'unfriend' him," Abby said.

"I'm not ready yet, but we're not going to think about Rob tonight. We're going to have fun. Jules and Char are meeting us there. How's the wedding planning going?" Rachel asked.

Abby groaned. "Can we put that in the same category as Rob tonight?"

Rachel laughed. "Fine with me."

The Hitching Post was hopping with business. With a football game playing on several of the flat-screen TVs, the bar area was crowded with guys rooting for their teams. Abby skimmed the bar/restaurant for Cade, and felt a pinch of disappointment when she didn't see him. *Get over it,* she told herself.

Jules and Char waved them over from a table on the far side of the room. "Woo-hoo," Char said, lifting her beer. "The chicks are out of the coop tonight." She lowered her voice. "Plus we've got a hot server. I think I should order a round for everyone, don't you?"

"I'm a lightweight, so I'll take water to start," Abby said.

"Me, too. I'm driving, so I don't want to take any chances," Rachel said.

Char frowned. "Okay, but I don't think he's going to like the tip he gets from water."

"We can order some food," Rachel suggested, grabbing a menu. "The ribs look good."

"Not for me," Abby said. "Those are LipSmackin' Ribs and I don't want to have anything to do with that company."

"Such passion about ribs," the server said from behind her and gave her a once-over, twice. "You could give their waitresses some competition."

Abby felt her cheeks heat with color. "I'm not interested in competing with LipSmackin' Ribs's waitresses. I would, however, like a hot-fudge sundae with whipped cream and nuts."

"Cherry on top?" he asked, and she saw a look of sexual interest in his gaze. After her recent depressing experiences with Cade, it gave her a little thrill. At least some males found her attractive.

"Yes, thank you," she said.

"What else can I get you lovely ladies?" he asked and took their order. "I'll be back," he said, looking deliberately at Abby.

"Ooh, he's definitely interested in you, Abby," Jules said. "And he's cute. Maybe you should hang out with him."

Abby felt conflicted. "I don't know. I'm really busy right now with school and ROOTS. This probably isn't a good time."

"When *is* a good time?" Rachel asked. "Come to think of it, you hardly ever give a guy a chance. Unless you're still holding out for—"

Abby shot Rachel the look of death, which thankfully caused her to close her mouth.

"Oops," Rachel said.

"Holding out for what?" Jules asked.

"Or who?" Char said.

A friend since junior high school, Rachel was one of the few people in the world in whom Abby had confided about her crush over Cade, and since Laila had started dating him, the two had made a deal not to discuss him unless Abby brought up the subject, which had been nearly never.

The server returned with their drinks and orders. He set her ice-cream sundae in front of her along with a piece of paper. "Text me," he invited, then turned to the rest of the group. "Anything else I can get you?"

"Three more just like you," Char said, flirting outrageously.

He chuckled. "I'll see what I can round up," he said and went to another table of customers.

"You have to text him," Jules said. "He's cute and I bet he would be a lot of fun. You could use a little fun."

"We'll see," she said. Maybe Jules was right. Maybe she shouldn't be spending all her time waiting for Cade. It's just that no other man had come close in her eyes.

"Speaking of fun, is anyone leaving town during the holidays?" Rachel asked. "I'm stuck here."

Abby shot Rachel a look of gratitude for taking the focus off of her, and the women discussed dreams of a trip to the Caribbean. It was all in fun. Abby visited the restroom and when she came out, her gaze collided with Cade's. Her heart immediately slammed into her ribs.

His gaze traveled up and down her and he gave her a slight nod before he turned back to the football game. She felt a shot of something like humiliation travel through her at his muted, unfriendly response. He might as well have snubbed her.

Indignation rose within her and she refused to let him get away with it. The last time she'd been with Cade, he'd been practically making love to her and she wasn't going to let him forget it that easily.

Stiffening her spine, she sauntered toward him and tapped him on the shoulder. "Nice to see you. How you been lately?" she asked and deliberately licked her lips.

"Okay," he said, barely sparing her a glance. "Been busy at the shop."

"Yeah, it's that season," she said. "It must get terribly *frustrating* being cooped up in that shop all day and night. I don't know how you do it."

"You do what you have to do," he said.

And she would, too, she told herself, taking her courage in her hands. "That beer looks good. You mind if I have a sip of yours?"

He glanced at her. "I thought you didn't like beer."

She shot him what she hoped was a seductive look. "I might like yours," she said.

He gave a muffled sigh and lifted the beer toward her. She lifted her hand at the same time and between the two of them, the mug was jiggled and cold liquid spilled onto her chest.

Abby gasped. She had not intended that to happen.

Cade swore under his breath. "Hey, give me some napkins," he said to the bartender. Seconds later, he was pressing them against her chest. "How the hell did that happen?" he muttered.

Abby's heart stuttered at his closeness, her body conjuring memories of how he'd caressed her and kissed her. "It's not the only thing that could happen again," she murmured.

He jerked his head upward and met her gaze. He looked at his hands and her chest for a long moment, then picked up one of her hands to give her the napkins while he backed away. "Go away, little girl."

His insistence on calling her a girl made her crazy. "You know very well I'm no little girl."

"This isn't going to work. Do you realize that I baby-sat for you once?" he asked.

Abby felt another wave of humiliation, but she pushed it aside. "That was one time and it wasn't really babysitting. It was a swimming camp and my mom asked if I could stay late because she had to take one of my sisters to the doctor."

"Close enough for me," he said. "You're too young and immature for me. I need a woman, not a girl."

Abby felt her anger explode like a Fourth of July firecracker. Straight through the roof. Her heart hammered like a shotgun that wouldn't stop. She narrowed her eyes at Cade, picked up his half-spilled beer and dumped the rest of it. In his lap.

His eyes widened. "What the—"

"That's what this woman does when she is roaring mad," Abby whispered. "Maybe you can remember the cold feeling down below when you start thinking about the fact that you want me more than you're willing to admit." Turning on her heel, she strode to the table where her friends were chatting and drinking.

Rachel glanced at her and her brow furrowed. "You okay?" she whispered.

"Never better," Abby said, adrenaline still coursing through her veins.

"You're lying," Rachel said, looking over Abby's shoulder. "What happened?"

"I just did something a sweet, good little girl wouldn't do," Abby said in a low voice, taking a sip of her water and wishing it was a martini.

"And that is?" Rachel asked.

"I poured half of Cade Pritchett's beer in his lap." The revelation was more satisfying than she could have ever expected.

Rachel gasped, then laughed—then laughed again. "You didn't?"

"I did," Abby said.

"Oh, I wish I could have seen that." Rachel lifted her hand for Abby to give a high five. "You just kicked butt. I can only hope I'll have enough guts to do the same thing to Rob."

"I didn't plan it," Abby said, feeling a sliver of guilt.

"Of course not," Rachel said.

"What are you two whispering about?" Char asked.

Abby paused a half beat, then manufactured an excuse. "I didn't want to tell everyone I was pooped. It's embarrassing."

"Hey, we're all overbooked with exams and papers," Char said. "We understand. Plus we can always insist you give a rain check. And maybe you can bring that server and a few of his friends with you."

For the first time in a long time, if not forever, Abby considered taking a chance on someone other than Cade since Cade was rejecting her completely. She didn't know how much humiliation she could take. Even now, she felt a twinge of regret for dumping Cade's beer in his lap. It wasn't her nature to be so impulsive and, well, aggressive.

Abby rubbed the piece of paper with her server's contact information between her fingers, wishing it were a lucky charm that would release her from her passion for Cade. "You never know," she finally said. "Anything is possible."

Cade couldn't believe sweet little Abby had dumped his beer in his lap. He stared after her as she returned to her table.

"Need some more napkins?" the bartender asked innocently.

"Yeah," Cade muttered. He didn't want to leave the bar with his pants so wet.

"And another beer?" the bartender asked as he gave Cade some napkins.

"Not right now," he said then swore under his breath. *Women.* Who would have thought Abby could be so impulsive? So emotional? So passionate and hot...

A slew of images and memories conspired against him, making him want to take her to his bed for at least a night. Or thirty nights.

All wrong, he reminded himself as he forced himself to remember that he had once been her babysitter. He had once been involved with her sister. Cade knew Abby would want more from him than he could give. Unlike Laila, Abby would want all of him. His mind, body and heart, and Cade had no intention of giving away all of himself to any woman.

A few days later, Cade walked toward the diner to get a decent cup of coffee since the coffeemaker at the shop had taken its last gasp. He ended up getting an extra cup for his brother Dean and headed back to work. Passing by the community center, he heard the sound of children singing. He remembered that the kids were preparing a Thanksgiving program and wondered if this was part of it.

He'd successfully avoided Abby since the incident at the Hitching Post. Her words, however, grated on him. It still wasn't acceptable for him to get involved with her. Abby had a soft heart and he would hurt her. Hell, he already had.

He hated himself for it, but he missed seeing her. He'd spent a lifetime not thinking about Abby, and now thoughts of her crept up in his mind at the oddest moments. Cade should just continue on his way back to the shop. No detours.

Or he could stand in the back where no one would notice him. Just to see if the props from Pritchett & Sons were working out okay. Sipping his coffee, he stepped inside the center and nodded at the woman at the desk as he made his way to the gymnasium.

It must have been a dress rehearsal because the kids were in costume. He had to admit they looked cute. A bunch of little pilgrims stood on the bow of the faux ship singing their little lungs out. One of the pilgrims pulled off her hat and started playing with it. In front of the ship, a group of mini–Native Americans wearing headdresses squirmed and wiggled. One little Native American started tugging on his neighbor's headdress.

He spied Abby stepping toward the tugger and shaking her head. The boy immediately stepped in line.

He chuckled. The boy must have learned, as Cade was learning, that despite her sweet smile and nature, Abby had a kick to her personality. The song about making friends and sharing ended, and Abby and the director applauded the children's efforts.

Cade knew that most of these preschoolers came from disadvantaged homes. Their time at the community center provided a hot meal, early education and exposure to learning all kinds of things they might never experience otherwise. With all her other activities, he had to admire Abby for helping the children.

As she bent down to untie a headdress, the children swarmed around her like bees to a flower. No surprise that she was good with kids. He felt the dark longing for his own family yawn inside him again and tamped it down. Maybe someday, but not with Abby. He would only hurt her.

Chapter Five

Between school, her work at ROOTS and filling in at the community center, Abby's schedule switched into high gear. In theory, she was too busy to think about Cade, but that's why theories were only theories. Real life was something else. The good news, however, was that she was too busy to be overly bothered with Laila's wedding. Sure, she felt a twinge every now and then, but with her current demands, it was easier to push aside.

After one of her night classes, she grabbed a hot chocolate with marshmallows at the diner while she sat in a booth and reviewed notes for an upcoming exam. A shadow fell over her and she glanced up to see the server from the Hitching Post looking down at her.

"You didn't call or text me," he said.

"I've been crazy busy with school and other things," she said.

"Too busy for a little fun?" he asked, sitting across from her.

"Too busy for any fun," she said.

"You don't remember my name," he said.

She searched her memory. *Started with a* D. "Daniel," she managed.

He raised his eyebrows. "Well done."

She shrugged, knowing she'd just gotten lucky and tried not to squirm at the way he studied her.

"I'm not just a waiter for the Hitching Post," he said. "I'll be studying law in the fall."

"I wasn't judging you," she rushed to say, although she was somewhat surprised.

"But you couldn't be less interested," he said.

She was impressed by his perceptiveness. "You're good," she said and pushed a strand of her hair behind her ear. "The truth is I'm cursed," she confessed.

His eyebrows lifted. "Cursed? That sounds a bit dramatic," he said.

"Well, it is dramatic, and I am, indeed, cursed. I fell head over heels for a man when I was a teenager, and even when I tried my very best not to care for him, I did. I failed at ignoring him. I failed at not thinking he was the best man in the world."

Disappointment flitted through his gaze. "Oh. Damn. How come no one like you went crazy for me as a teenager and couldn't be seduced away?"

"Ha, ha. I'm sure there were plenty of girls falling

for you. You just probably didn't notice them because there were so many. You're not exactly hard to look at, and you're full of charm."

"Not enough charm to turn your head," he said.

Abby sighed. "I'm just sick. It's a sad thing, but I'm sick."

"You should give me a chance," Daniel said. "Maybe I could cure you."

She laughed, wishing she felt remotely tempted, and shook her head. "Maybe not me, but I could refer you to at least eight of my friends if you promised not to break their hearts."

"Eight at once and no hearts broken? That's a tall order," he joked.

She laughed, again wishing her heart were as free as it should be. Free enough to enjoy and exchange interest with another man. Darn Cade Pritchett. Why had he captured her heart if he would never return her feelings?

The weather forecast was wicked bad. Blizzard coming. Fifteen inches. Zero visibility. Abby thought about Mr. Henson. She'd packaged several meals from the Cateses' freezer and taken them to him several days ago, but she hadn't checked on him recently.

Guilt slashed through her. She should have visited him. She should have… Well, no more should haves. She would go check on him now before the storm hit full force.

Abby drove her VW Beetle as the snow was flying.

She pulled in to Mr. Henson's driveway with more food and rushed up the steps to knock on his door.

"Coming," he called from inside.

Abby waited impatiently, glancing at the snow pouring sideways.

Mr. Henson opened the door and smiled. "What are you doing here?" he asked, his grumpy tone at odds with his expression.

"I wanted to make sure you're okay," she said. "A blizzard is coming and I brought you some more food."

"I like your mama's cooking," he said. "Yours isn't too bad, either," he added, waving her inside. "You shouldn't have come out in this weather."

Abby stepped inside. "I was worried about you."

"No need to worry about me. I'll go when I'm supposed to and—"

"—not a day before," she finished for him. "I just don't want you rushing things."

He met her gaze. "Why is that?"

"I like you."

His lips lifted in a small, craggy smile. "You shouldn't get too hung up on me. My Geraldine told me I was dangerous to women. I never believed it, but—"

Abby stifled a laugh, but smiled. "Geraldine was right. How's your ankle?"

"Damn slow healing," he said as he shuffled toward the kitchen. "If I was just a few years younger, I'd be better fast, like that," he said and snapped his fingers. "This one is taking a while. Gotta say the ice and meds help a little. A *little,*" he added with emphasis. "It's no miracle."

"I hope you'll turn a corner soon. I'm glad you're not hurting quite as much. In the meantime, I want to make sure you're ready for this blizzard headed our way."

Mr. Henson lifted his head as if he were offended. "I've lived through more blizzards than years you've been alive, missy."

"I'm sure you have," she said. "But I'm a neurotic whippersnapper who wants to make sure you make it through this one, too."

He stared at her for a long moment. "This younger generation is strange."

A knock sounded at the door, startling both of them. "I'll get it," she said and strode toward the door. She opened it, stunned to see Cade staring back at her. Her heart felt as if it lodged in her throat.

"What are you doing here?" she and Cade said at the same time.

Abby blinked, reining in her heart, mind and soul. *Oh, not soul,* she told herself. Not soul. That was too much, too deep. "I'm here because of the blizzard."

"So am I," Cade said. "You shouldn't be here. It's already started."

"My car is good in the snow," she said, lifting her chin.

Cade gave a short, humorless laugh. "In this weather? I don't think so."

"It is," she insisted. "I wouldn't have come out here if my car couldn't have made it."

"Yeah, well, good luck making it back. The visibility is already shot," Cade said.

Abby frowned. Now she was dealing with two grumpy old men.

Cade walked past her. "You need some wood? What's your flashlight and candle situation?" he asked Mr. Henson.

"What's wrong with you two? I've been through blizzards before. I can do it again," he said.

"But your ankle," she said.

Cade glanced back at her. "What about his ankle?"

"He sprained and bruised it. I took him to the doctor last week."

"It's nothing," Mr. Henson said. "But the ice and meds helped. I'm fine."

"Why didn't you tell me?" Cade asked.

"You weren't talking with me," she retorted. "I'm too young to know anything. Remember?"

Silence fell over the room. They could have heard a pin drop.

"Hmm," Cade said and turned back to Mr. Henson. "Let's double-check your supplies, heat and cell phone. I need to make sure Abby gets home okay."

"I'm good. You get your woman home," Mr. Henson said.

Abby groaned.

"*My* woman?" Cade echoed. "She's not my woman."

"Well, she would be if you had any sense," Mr. Henson said. "Do you know what a good cook she is? She's brought me some meals."

Cade shrugged his shoulders. "I didn't know. Glad she's been feeding you."

"You know, it's a mighty fine thing when a woman can cook like she does. That's part of what makes a good wife. Plus she's doggone pretty. Have you taken a good look at her? She's—"

"Mr. Henson," Abby said, feeling her cheeks blaze with embarrassment. "We really do want to make sure you're going to be okay during this storm." She cleared her throat. "Batteries," she said. "I'll check the batteries."

Within a few moments, she and Cade had Mr. Henson armed and prepared for the storm. "Now, you take care and I'll check on you again. Call if you have any problems," she said, squeezing the elderly man's shoulders.

"I won't have any problems," he told her.

"Then call for any reason," she said. "I should go." Resisting the urge to meet Cade's gaze, she pulled on her gloves and strode out of the house.

Cade had been telling the truth about the weather. The white stuff was pouring down with a vengeance. She adjusted her cap and swiped the snow out of her eyes as she stomped to her car. Her VW started up with its usual dependability and she flipped on the windshield wipers to the fastest setting. Putting the car into gear, she pushed the accelerator and slowly moved forward.

The visibility was terrible, but Abby figured if she went slow and steady, she would be okay. Fishtailing up Mr. Henson's driveway didn't build her confidence, but she soldiered on. It was only about twenty miles between Mr. Henson's house and her home, she told herself and kept a light foot on the accelerator.

Soon enough, she saw Cade's SUV in her rearview mirror. Certain she was moving too slowly for him, she opened her window and waved her hand for him to pass, but he didn't. Of course not, she thought. He had to look after her the same way he would look after his little sister. Having him at her backside just made her more edgy, especially when her little VW pulled left when she was holding the steering wheel straight.

Moving at a snail's pace, she wrapped her hands around the steering wheel with a death grip. Suddenly another car appeared out of nowhere and headed straight for the driver's side of her VW. Her heart raced and panic rushed through her. Abby swung the steering wheel to the right and mashed on the accelerator. The snow was so thick she was driving blind. She felt it the second her car lost traction with the road and pitched downward, then collided with something that brought her car to a halt, her seat belt jerking her tightly against her seat. She held her breath and squished her eyes together, waiting for the air bag to slap her.

When it didn't, she slowly opened her eyes and took a careful breath and did a quick physical evaluation. She jiggled her arms and legs and—

A thump sounded on her window, scaring the bejeezus out of her. Abby looked out the window into Cade's concerned gaze. Her heart turned over. Blast it.

"Are you okay?" he yelled.

She nodded. "Fine. Really," she called in return. "I can handle it. I'm okay."

He shook his head and motioned for her to roll down her window.

"I'm fine. Really," she repeated as she lowered her window. "I can handle this."

"You're in a ditch," he said.

"Oh," she said. "Oops."

"Unlock the door. I'll help you up to my car," he said.

She didn't like the put-upon sound in his voice. "I could call my father," she said.

"There's no need for him to come get you when I'm here," he said.

"I don't want you to feel obligated," she said. "You feel obligated to rescue everyone. I don't want you to feel obligated about me."

"Open the door," he said. "It's damn cold out here."

"Charming," she muttered under her breath, but did as he said. He extended his hand and she accepted it, wishing he was reaching for her in entirely different circumstances. That was a dream that wasn't going to come true anytime soon.

Pulling her hand from his, she climbed up the side of the ditch. She tripped once and he reached out his hand, but she ignored it. She trudged upward and made it to the top where Cade's SUV blinked its emergency lights at her in an almost mocking way. Abby resisted the urge to stick her tongue out at the vehicle, knowing her attitude was ridiculous.

Cade led the way to the passenger side of his vehicle and opened the door. She stepped inside, reluctantly grateful for the warmth. Cade climbed into the driver's seat.

"You shouldn't have gone out to old man Henson's house in the middle of a blizzard," he said.

"It wasn't the middle of a blizzard," she retorted. "It was the beginning."

"Same thing," he said. "Why didn't you call me?"

"Why should I?" she asked. "You told me I was too young. That means nothing I say is valid."

"I didn't say that," he began.

"Same thing," she countered and crossed her arms over her chest.

Silence followed, and she refused to fill it, though she wondered if it would kill her. This was going to be the longest ride of her life.

He could smell her perfume. It wasn't strong, but soft and flowery with a hint of spice. Cade told himself he should ignore it, but his nose must have thought differently because he inhaled more deeply. Lord, she smelled good. He stole a sideways glance at her and immediately caught the stubborn set of her jaw so at odds with her soft, overly full mouth.

Her lips could conjure wicked images in a man's mind. Not his, of course, he told himself. Abby was the equivalent of his second little sister. Off-limits.

He saw her lick her lips and his gut tightened. Those wicked images began to seep through his brain like smoke through a keyhole. Cade gritted his teeth and focused on the road.

"I would listen to you about Mr. Henson. I know you've got a good head on your shoulders," he said.

"Hmmph."

"Really," he said. "Look at all you're doing for the community center and ROOTS. You're close to graduating." He paused and took a breath. "You're an intelligent young woman."

She shot him a gaze full of doubt.

Cade tore his gaze away from her sexy mouth. "You are," he insisted and took a deep breath. "You and I just shouldn't get involved."

"And why is that? If I'm an intelligent young woman?" she asked in a quiet voice.

"Because—" He bit his tongue to keep from saying she was too young and inexperienced. "Because underneath it all, I'm a heartless sonovabitch and I'll hurt you."

Her shocked silence was so thick he could have cut it with a knife.

"I find that difficult to believe," she finally said. "I've known you for a long time and I don't know anyone who would call you a heartless sonovabitch."

"You don't know anyone I've ever fallen in love with, do you?" he challenged, tightening his hands on the steering wheel.

Another silence stretched between them. "Laila," she finally said.

"No. Laila and I were never in love. I haven't been

capable of love for a long time, Abby. You're not rough and hard like me. You should have someone who can love as freely as you can."

Abby didn't say anything in return as she appeared to digest his words. Instead of talking, she turned on his radio to a classic-rock station and turned up the heat in his SUV a notch.

Aeons later, he pulled into her driveway. Abby turned to him. "You wouldn't want me to make decisions for you. Don't make decisions for me," she said in a soft voice. "And I'm sorry I poured that beer in your lap the other night. It was impulsive, even though you kinda deserved it." She leaned toward him, close enough to kiss him.

He felt a crazy, wicked expectancy swell inside him and waited. And wanted.

"Thanks," she whispered, pulling back and getting out of his car. He looked after her, swearing at himself because he was hard with wanting her. Forbidden fruit was a pain in the butt.

He had warned her off. If anyone was advising Abby, they would say to stay away from Cade Pritchett, but her thoughts gravitated toward him despite the fact that she was crazy busy. He should have been the last thing on her mind, but he wasn't. Abby did her best to make sure he wasn't the first, but he was right up there.

Even though he'd warned her away from him, she'd seen the way he'd looked at her mouth. He'd almost wanted her to kiss him. Almost. So, he *was* attracted to her. She had to keep reminding herself because he'd discouraged her every time she'd approached him. Every time she'd tried to seduce him. Which had felt like a joke because she didn't know anything about seduction. The only thing Abby knew was that she had wanted Cade as long as she could remember.

But she wasn't sure she could put herself out there again. It was so humiliating wanting him to notice her as a woman, wanting him to want her just half as much as she wanted him. She'd seen the spark, though, and a part of her couldn't help but hope that spark could turn into a fire between Cade and her. If only the two of them could get together again with no one else around. Just the two of them and maybe, just maybe she would get the chance she'd been waiting for since forever.

Abby waited several more days, hoping she would run into Cade, but that didn't happen. At this rate, it looked as if she would have to seek him out if she was going to see him before next year. Taking matters into her own hands, she headed for Pritchett & Sons near closing time. Just before 6:00 p.m., she walked into the display area and found Cade putting holiday decorations into the window.

He met her gaze then looked away. "Hey," he said.

Abby shoved her hands into the pockets of her jacket at his cool tone. She had her work cut out for her. "Hey to you. Bet you've been busy lately," she said and walked toward him.

"Always busy this time of year," he said, carefully placing a nutcracker on the middle shelf.

She nodded. "Yep." She bent down and picked up another nutcracker. "My mother loves these. She collects them."

"I know," he said.

Of course he knew, she thought. He'd dated Laila for several years that had included several Christmas seasons. "I think there's something creepy about them."

He glanced at her in surprise. "Really? Why?"

"I think it's the combination of inanimate eyes and a jaw that can crack nuts. It reminds me of Chucky in that horror movie *Child's Play*."

"They're not that spooky," he said and bent down to put another nutcracker on the shelf.

"Easy for you to say," she said. "Did one of your older sisters ever whack you on the head with one of them?"

He shot her a sideways glance. "Not Laila," he said.

"Yes, Miss Perfect Laila," she said, revealing a bit more bitterness than she intended.

"She's not perfect," he said in a mild voice. "That wasn't why I proposed to her."

"You proposed because she was the most beautiful woman in Thunder Canyon," she said.

"Most beautiful is relative. I proposed because I thought she was strong enough to deal with me. You know, despite getting whacked with a nutcracker, you're lucky you have your family. Especially when the holidays come around."

"I guess," she said and picked up an ornament that resembled a snow-covered church. She giggled as she held up the ornament.

"What?" Cade asked.

"Do you remember when Reverend Walker's mother blew up her kitchen just before Christmas?"

Cade nodded with a smile. "She was making moonshine."

"My mother didn't stop talking about that for months," she said and giggled again. "I love Christmas."

She felt his gaze on her and looked up at him. He glanced away. "What about you?"

"It's a mixed bag," he said with a shrug. "I have some happy memories, but ever since my mother died, it's hard. Sometimes it's just a day to get through."

Abby's heart twisted at the pain in his voice. "That's got to be difficult."

"That's why I said you're lucky. You still have your family intact."

Grabbing hold of her courage, she took a quick breath. "You could have your own family if that was what you really wanted. You just have to reach out for it."

Cade met her gaze for a long moment, and she saw the hunger in his eyes, the same hunger she felt for him. He leaned toward her and lifted his hand, then pulled back at the last second as if coming to his senses.

"You don't know what you're talking about. I'm not right for you," he said.

Frustration roared through her, making her want

to stomp her foot and scream, which she suspected wouldn't help her cause. "Says who? Shouldn't I get a say in the matter? I'm starting to wonder if you're afraid of how you feel for me."

"I'm not afraid," he said in a low voice, but she saw something different flash through his gaze. A strong flicker of passion she hadn't seen before. Abby took a step closer, then another and lifted her hand to his arm, sliding it upward to his shoulder. She gently pressed her chest against his and watched him close his eyes and take a quick, sharp breath.

"Doesn't this feel right?" she whispered and lifted her other hand to his other shoulder.

Moving in achingly slow increments, he slid his hands around her, pulling her into his arms. Her heart pounded in her chest and her lungs refused to work. Cade's stormy gaze met hers and she could tell he was still fighting his feelings. "I shouldn't be the one to take your innocence."

"You won't be. I'm more grown-up than you think," she assured him and lifted on tiptoes to press her mouth against his. She slid her tongue over the seam of his lips, and he immediately took her mouth in a hungry kiss.

It was as if a dam inside him broke loose. She felt his hands on her hair, against her back, pushing her into his hard crotch. Breathless, hot and filled with need, she matched him kiss for kiss, caress for caress.

He pulled back slightly and swore. "Are you sure about this?"

"Yes," she said before he could finish the question.

He took her mouth again in a quick, hard kiss that promised so much more. "I'd better lock the door."

Chapter Six

Cade cut the lights and led her to a room in the back. "We can have some privacy here," he said and closed the door behind them. A big sofa faced an old television, and at the far end of the room sat a small table and chairs with a refrigerator and microwave. "This is where we rest when we're pulling all-nighters," he said.

Her heart skipped as he laced his fingers through hers and guided her toward the sofa. She couldn't help hoping they would be pulling a different kind of all-nighter tonight.

He slid his fingers through her hair and she automatically lifted her mouth to his again. He kissed her deeply, and the fire between them flared again. Now that he was so close, she couldn't get enough of him fast enough. She tugged at his shirt, pulling the buttons free, dipping her open mouth against his throat to catch a breath. His ragged breathing was music to her ears.

With his assistance, she finally peeled off the layers covering his upper body and slid her hands over his muscular chest. He was all man. She wanted to feel all of him against all of her. She rubbed her chest and mouth over his bare skin and he shuddered.

Unable to fight her impatience, she pulled off her sweater and tossed it over her head. When she reached to remove her bra, his hands replaced hers and that barrier was gone in seconds.

She moaned in pleasure at the sensation of her bare breasts rubbing against his chest. His groan joined hers. "You feel so good."

"I'm gonna make you feel good, too," she promised and slid her hands down to unbuckle his belt and undo his jeans. She filled her hands with him and he whispered another oath.

"Where did you learn—"

She pressed her mouth against his and began to stroke him. Now was not the time for questions. Now was the time for pure pleasure. The heat between them built so quickly she would have sworn it was summertime. When he grazed her nipples with his thumbs, she felt a corresponding tug low between her thighs.

She bit her lip at the sensations ripping through her. "I want you."

"Not too fast," he said. "Not too—"

She stroked him intimately again and he sucked

in another sharp breath. "What are you trying to do to me?"

"The same thing you do to me," she said. "Fast isn't fast enough."

With a rough groan, he stripped off the rest of her clothes and nudged her onto the sofa. He stood directly in front of her and she pushed his jeans and underwear down then gave him an intimate kiss.

It didn't last long. Seconds later, he followed her down on the couch, pushing her legs apart with his thigh. He dipped his fingers into the place where she was aching for him.

"You're already wet," he said in approval as he caressed her and made her more restless for him. Each stroke made her a little more crazy.

"Inside," she whispered. "Come inside."

Three more delicious, mind-bending strokes and it seemed he couldn't wait any longer. He thrust inside her and she arched toward him. She felt his gaze fall over her like liquid fire. The want in his eyes nearly pushed her over the top. When he began to move, she moved in return. The sensations inside her built and she clung to him. He thrust again and she felt herself spin out of control. A heartbeat later, she felt him stiffen with his own climax and she relished the fact that for this moment, this night, he was finally hers.

Cade stared at the lithe temptress in his arms while he tried to catch his breath. Little Abby Cates. Who would have known she was wild in bed? She met his gaze and her lips lifted in a sensual smile that reminded him of a cat who'd just licked a bowl of cream. Her hands slid over his skin with sensual strokes that indicated she wouldn't be adverse to going round two with him.

Cade, however, wanted to get control of himself and he was curious as hell about Abby Firecracker Cates. She was a lot more experienced than he'd expected and not at all shy about going after what she wanted. It made him wonder how many men… A shot of jealousy burned through him, taking him by surprise. He shifted, sitting up slightly, and pulled her onto his lap.

"You took me by surprise," he said, sliding his fingers through her hair, which skimmed the top of her breasts. Gazing down her naked body, he thought about everything he still wanted to do to her.

"How is that?" she asked.

"Well, I don't know. I didn't think you'd be so—" He broke off. "I though you would be more shy. Not so experienced."

She licked her lips. "Are you saying you didn't like—"

"Hell, no," he said and raked his hand through his hair. "I just— How many guys have you dated, anyway?"

She smiled. "Oh, well I've been out with a lot of guys, but I've only really been with one other guy. First year in college. One time," she said and turned her head away as if she embarrassed to discuss it.

"One time?" he echoed, incredulous. "You didn't

make love with me like you'd only done it one other time."

Abby sighed and looked at him, sliding her hands over his chest in a way that made him begin to get aroused again. "Okay, I'll tell you my secret," she whispered and rubbed her mouth against his. "You inspire me."

A ripple of pleasure raced through him like lit gasoline. No one had ever said anything so sexy to him in his life.

An hour later, after they'd made love again, Cade knew he would sleep well tonight. In fact, he could fall into a half coma given half a chance.

"I should take you home," he said, sliding his hands through her hair. He could get addicted to the silky sensation.

"No need. My car's parked down the street," she said.

"I can't let you drive home by yourself," he said, his innate sense of protectiveness rising to the surface.

"That would be crazy since I have my car," she said, rising and beginning to put on her clothes. "But it's a nice thought."

Cade felt a strange combination of feelings. He didn't want her to leave, yet he needed to get himself together. This had been a wild few hours that he hadn't expected.

"This doesn't seem right," he said, pulling on his own clothes.

"It's okay," she said, then paused and a flicker of vulnerability flashed through her eyes. "Is this a one-night stand?" she asked in a low voice.

Cade paused. It should be a one-night stand, he thought. But it wouldn't be. Abby had burrowed her way inside him and he couldn't let her go. Right now, anyway. "No," he said standing. "It's not a one-night stand."

Relief trickled through her expression, and he could practically feel the tension ease from her frame. "Then everything's okay," she said and pulled on her boots. "And I, um, guess I'll see you when I see you," she said, meeting his gaze with a smile.

She was fully dressed and somehow much more grown-up to him than she had been mere hours ago. She was a woman.

"I'll walk you to your car," he said and pulled on the rest of his clothes. He grabbed his jacket and led the way out the back room, then out of the shop. The frigid air hit him like a slap in the face.

"Whoa," he said. "It's doggone cold."

"Can't disagree," she said, snuggling inside her coat.

He reached over and put his arm around her. "Sure you're okay driving yourself home. This doesn't seem right."

"I'll be okay," she said.

"So, you wanna get together Wednesday?" he asked.

"Not good for me. I have a study group that night."

"Thursday?"

"Babysitting for my ROOTS mom Lisa," she said.

"Well, can you squeeze me in on Friday?" he asked in a half-mocking voice.

"Maybe," she said, fluttering her eyelids in a flirty way.

His gut clenched. Frowning, he wondered where that sensation had come from. "Friday," he said firmly.

"Where?" she asked.

"My house," he said. "And I"ll pick you up."

"It would be better if I drive. That way I won't get any questions."

"I can handle questions," he said.

"There's no need right now," she said and before they knew it, her orange VW was in sight.

"You should be driving a more substantial vehicle," he grumbled.

"My car gets me around," she said.

"And into ditches," he said.

"One ditch," she corrected. "Durring a blizzard. I've never gotten stuck before."

"If you say so," he said as they stopped beside her car. He lifted his hands and cradled her hand between them. "I'll see you Friday," he said and lowered his mouth to hers. Her lips were swollen from their passion. They quickly grew warm. He did, too. He slid his hand lower to the small of her back to draw her against him where she made him ache for her. Even after all their lovemaking.

That kiss went on and on, and he would have extended it longer if he hadn't needed oxygen. He drew back and they both gasped for air. Cade laughed uneasily. He couldn't remember the last time a woman had affected him this way. Had Dominique?

"All righty," she finally said in a sexy, husky voice. "I guess I should go."

"Yeah," he said, but still held her in his arms.

"I don't really want to," she confessed in a whisper.

"That makes two of us," he said. "I'll get my SUV and follow you home."

"Not necessary," she said.

"It is for me," he said and gave her a brief, firm kiss and pulled back.

"G'night," she said softly, and he helped her into her car.

Jogging back to the shop, Cade got into his SUV and quickly caught up with Abby on her drive toward her home. As he drove, he remembered all the other times he'd taken this same route to get together with Laila. That seemed centuries ago. Although Cade had never been in love with Laila, Abby had completely wiped Laila out of his mind.

He turned onto her street and watched as she pulled to a stop. Lowering her window, she peeked outside. "See you soon, Cade," she said with a wave.

Cade waved in return, feeling a little crazy.

Abby sauntered into the warm kitchen of her home where Laila and her mother were making lists and looking at photographs of bridesmaid dresses. Humming under her breath, she tried to withhold her giddiness over the evening she'd shared with Cade. Plus, she would see him again soon. She was so happy she almost couldn't contain herself, yet at the same time, she wanted to keep the fantastic news to herself a bit longer.

"Hey, Abby," Laila said. "What do you think of this bridesmaid dress? It's not too fussy, is it?"

It was horribly fussy and the color was hideous. "Oh, it's pretty."

"What about this one?" she asked, pointing to a pink dress with lace.

"Oh, that's pretty, too. Is there anything around here to eat?"

"You didn't have any dinner, did you?" her mother asked, frowning. "Where have you been, sweetie?"

Abby felt her cheeks heat and swiped at her hair. "Regular thing. Studying."

Feeling Laila scrutinize her, Abby turned away. "I'll just fix myself a peanut-butter-and-jelly sandwich."

"There's some chicken potpie in the refrigerator," her mother said.

"The wind must have picked up outside," Laila said. "Your hair's a mess."

Her hair was a mess because Cade couldn't keep his hands out of it, she thought, remembering how he'd tugged at her hair to draw her mouth against his. She bit her lip and began to make her sandwich. "It always gets difficult to manage when I wait too long to get a haircut. I should make an appointment."

"Hmm," Laila said. "Hey, do you mind taking a look at just one more dress and telling me what you think."

"No problem," she said, licking a dot of grape jelly

from her finger. She looked over Laila's shoulder at the photo where's Laila's perfect fingernail pointed at a putrid green dress with rainbow-colored lace and a bustle. It was one of the most hideous dresses she'd ever seen in her life. *But who cares?* she thought. She'd be happy to wear a burlap sack as long as Cade held her the way he had tonight. "Pretty again," she said and took a bite of her sandwich.

Laila shot her a look of complete suspicion. "What have you been smoking? That dress is awful."

Abby shrugged. "I hear it's bad luck to disagree with the bride."

"And what is your honest opinion?"

"My honest opinion is that this is your wedding and you should be happy with all of it," Abby said. "I'm going to grab a glass of milk and hit the sack soon. I'll see you later," she said and kissed her mother on the cheek.

Her mother sniffed. "Is that a new perfume you're wearing? I can't quite place it."

Abby felt a nervous twist and giggled. "Eau de *pbj?* G'night. Love ya."

Abby gulped down her sandwich and milk, then washed her face and brushed her teeth. Stripping out of her clothes, she put on her pj's. She picked up her shirt and inhaled, smelling a hint of Cade's scent—a delicious combination of aftershave, leather and pure man.

Her bedroom door swung open and Laila stepped inside, studying her. "What are you doing?"

Abby glanced away. "Smelling my shirt to see if I can get another day's wear out it. What do you think?"

"I don't know," Laila said. "There's something about you. I can't quite put my finger on it. You're practically—hmm—glowing. What's going on?" she demanded.

"Nothing. How are you doing? You seem to be making progress with your wedding plans," Abby said.

Laila furrowed her brow. "Don't change the subject." She frowned then her eyes rounded. "You've been with Cade. *What* have you been doing with him, Abby?"

"Nothing terrible," she said, because it had all been wonderful. "Why do you care? It's none of your business. You don't want him anymore. You never did," she said, her stomach clenching nervously.

"I care because you're my sister." Laila crossed the room and sat on Abby's bed. She lifted her hand to push a strand of Abby's hair from her face. "I know I said it was perfect if you and Cade got together, but I hope you won't move too fast with him. Or expect too much from him."

"What do you mean?" Abby asked, feeling a yucky sensation in her stomach.

"I mean, you're not that experienced."

"Oh, don't you start with that, too," Abby said, pulling back and rolling her eyes.

"Ah, so Cade has said the same thing," Laila said.

"I'm really tired," Abby said, not wanting to hear what her sister had to say. She'd had a magical evening, the most wonderful evening of her life, and she didn't want anyone, especially Laila, to spoil it. "I need to get some rest."

"Just be careful," Laila said. "Cade is a wonderful man, but when it comes to his heart, it may as well be locked up in Fort Knox."

"How would you know that?" Abby asked. "You never really took him seriously, anyway."

"But I've known him a long time," Laila said. "Like I said, Cade's a good man, but I don't want you to get hurt."

Abby sighed and put her hand over Laila's. "You had your chance with Cade and you didn't want him. Maybe that's why he never really opened up his heart to you. You didn't love him as much as—"

Laila's eyes rounded. "Oh, Abby. You may have a bad case of hero worship, but you can't be in love with him. You're too young."

Abby's frustration ripped through her. "I realize you're in love, but that doesn't make you an authority on my feelings, or Cade's." She smiled. "Be happy for me. I am. Just please don't tell anyone else. It's still too new," she said and sank back onto her pillow.

"What does *too new* mean?" Laila asked.

"Exactly what I said. Can you please keep it to yourself?" Abby asked.

"Yeah," Laila said in a reluctant but gentle voice and stroked Abby's head. "Just be careful with your sweet heart. And remember you deserve a man who can give you all of his heart, too. G'night, sweetie," she said and turned off the lamp beside Abby's bed.

In the darkness, Abby closed her eyes, wanting to close her mind to everything Laila had said. Laila may have dated Cade off and on for several years, but their relationship had never been deep. Abby shoved her sister's warnings out of her mind and focused on how Cade had felt in her arms, and how much he had wanted her. Surely, that had to mean something. With all his reservations, Cade wouldn't have given in to his feelings for her if those feelings weren't strong. Abby clung to that thought, but her sister's voice played through her mind like a song she wanted to forget.

Cade's fingers itched to call Abby several times during the next few days. He was torn between wanting to get together with her before Friday and telling her that the two of them together was not a good idea. He held off until Friday when his father came down with a virus, which wouldn't have been a big deal if a reporter for a major decorating magazine wasn't coming to town to interview his dad.

At the last minute, Cade was stuck answering three thousand questions from a snap-happy journalist. In the back of his mind, he noticed the time passing, but the journalist was fascinated with their specialty pieces and the stories behind them. At six o'clock, the journalist/reporter, Ellie Ogburn, offered to take him to dinner. Cade sent a text to Abby canceling their date, telling her he had a big work issue.

At the Hiching Post, Ellie continued to interview him. She was a lively, confident woman in her late twenties with an inquisitive mind. "So, how did you become such an artist? From my initial phone interview with your father, he said you were artistic from the beginning."

Uneasy with the woman's flattery, he scrubbed his chin with his palm. "My dad was being kind. In the beginning, my creativity didn't always mesh with functionality."

"Yes, your father encouraged you. So he must have seen a spark of genius?"

Cade winced. "I think *genius* is pushing it. You need to remember my family is all about hard work. All of us show up every day to get the job done."

"But you're the one in demand now. You're the one who makes the specialty pieces that everyone wants signed. Why?" she asked.

He shrugged. "I can't explain it. I just listen to the stories of why these clients want specialty pieces, and then I go to work. Sometimes it's about family. Sometimes it's about work, but it always involves some kind of passion. I think about the personalities of the people who are requesting these specialized pieces. The woodworking is important to them or they wouldn't be seeking me out. If you want something basic, you can go to a big-box store to take care of it. There's nothing wrong with that. This economy is squeezing all of us. But if you come to me asking for a customized piece, then I'm going to do my best to give you something unique that fits you and your needs."

Ellie smiled. "That's pretty impressive. You mentioned the word *passion*. Where's the passion in your life? Do you have anyone special that inspires you?" she asked, batting her eyelashes at him.

Her flirty response gave him a jolt, and his mind slid to thoughts of Abby. He couldn't help remembering when she'd told him that he inspired her. "I keep my personal life private," he said and just let his statement sit there. He could deal with the silence, but he'd learned that many other people couldn't.

Ellie nodded and finally said, "Okay, well, is there a Mrs. Cade Pritchett?"

"Not gonna discuss my private life," he said firmly.

"That's just a status," she protested. "Single or married."

"Last time," he said. "I'm not discussing my private life."

"That's a shame. Any chance you'd like to come to New York for a long weekend?" she asked.

"I wouldn't want to cloud the article you're going to write from this interview," he said.

She pursed her lips. "You're no fun."

"True," he said. "Ask anyone. I'm no fun."

"Why do I think that's a front?"

He shrugged, his mind sliding toward Abby. "No idea."

An hour later, he escorted Ellie to her hotel, but left before she entered the lobby. He drove home and entered his too-silent house. His dog greeted him with a bark and a wag then followed him as he walked to the kitchen to grab a beer. If things had ended out differently, as he'd planned, he wouldn't have spent the evening alone. His body warmed at the thought. She would have gotten him hot and taken him up and down and all around. She would have made him needy, but left him satisfied.

She was nowhere close, right now, though. He checked his cell phone for the tenth time for her response, but there was none. He wondered why she hadn't replied and decided he should shrug it off.

Cade took a beer from the fridge, popped it open and took a long gulp. What a day. He felt as if he'd been probed and prodded every which way. In any other situation, he would have walked away, but this had been business. This article could bring in big business. He especially hadn't liked it when the discussion had veered toward his personal passion. Cade didn't spend a lot of time thinking about personal passions. In fact, he avoided anything or anyone that got him too worked up. He'd fallen in love once, and that woman had died. On top of that, the woman who had made family happen for his brothers, sister and father, had died suddenly, taking away the whole concept of family happiness with her. Since then, Cade had felt half-dead inside. He'd still longed for his own family, but without the terrible pain he'd experienced when he was younger.

He checked his phone one more time. No messages, text or voice, from Abby. Maybe it was for the best.

Cade worked all day with his brother Dean on Saturday to make up for the time he spent with the reporter on Friday. The two of them finally took off for a late dinner at the Hitching Post after seven.

"I'm getting too much of this place," he said. "I'm going to DJ's for some good ribs next time I eat out."

"You didn't like Ellie?" Dean asked. "I thought she was hot."

"She was tiring," Cade said, sipping his beer and surveying the bar. "I'm glad you and I made good progress today. Her interview really cut into my time yesterday."

"Man, you're getting old if you think she was tiring. I wish you would have handed her over to me," Dean said.

"That interview could mean a lot for us. I wouldn't want you cluttering it because you wanted a good time. You can get a good time with a lot of women. No need to piss off this one," he said.

"And you think you didn't piss her off?" Dean asked, starting his second beer. "She looked like she wanted more than dinner with you."

"I dropped her off at her hotel and went home. I'm not a complete fool," Cade said.

"Tell the truth," Dean said. "You wouldn't have minded going up to her room, would you?"

The truth was Cade hadn't been at all interested, but he wasn't going to tell Dean that. "You gonna come into the shop tomorrow after church?"

Dean blanched. "I gotta go to church?"

Cade laughed. "Leona Moseley was asking about you the last time I went."

Dean groaned. "No way. She's been after me for two

years. Why do you think I don't go to church without someone to protect me? It's enough to make a man lose his religion."

Cade laughed again. "We all have to take turns. I took a turn two weeks ago. Dad is sick, so someone else needs to step up."

"Have some pity, Cade," Dean said. "I don't want to face Leona."

Cade groaned, but heard the sound of a familiar laugh from across the room. He tilted his head then searched the room. Nothing. Nothing. Noth— Cade's gaze collided with the sight of Abby with a group of girls and a guy with his arm wrapped around her waist.

A wicked twist of jealousy wrapped around his gut and throat like a python. What the hell was she doing here? What the hell was that guy doing touching her like that?

Chapter Seven

Abby forced herself to laugh at everyone's jokes. The sound she made was hollow to her own ears, but she focused on being amused instead of heartbroken. She laughed at another comment one of her friends made, although she couldn't repeat what made it so funny.

Daniel squeezed her waist. "You want to meet me after my shift?" he asked. "We could go out."

"That's too late for this schoolgirl," she said. "I have a ton of work to do."

"So you're blowing me off again," he said. "I could give you a good time."

"Maybe she doesn't want to have a good time with you right now. Or anytime," Cade said, taking Abby completely by surprise.

She dropped her jaw in surprise.

"Hey," Daniel said. "The lady can decide for herself."

"Well?" Cade said expectantly.

She narrowed her eyes at him for a long moment. How could he be so arrogant when he'd stood her up last night?

"You were pretty busy last night," she said then lowered her voice to a whisper. "With another woman."

"What did you say?" Cade asked, wrinkling his brow in confusion.

"You heard what I said," she hissed.

"I didn't," Cade said.

"Well, use your imagination. You were having dinner with a woman. One of my friends sent me a cell-phone photo of you enjoying a meal with a pretty woman last night when you told me you were working."

Realization flooded Cade's face. "That was the reporter. My father was supposed to handle this interview, but he got sick."

"Uh-huh," she said, unable to conceal her disbelief. "It must have been a real hardship to spend the evening with her."

"Hey, maybe I'd better take Abby home," Daniel said. "She seems upset and you're not helping any," he said to Cade.

Cade's face hardened with anger. "Not tonight, or any night for that matter." He took Abby's hand in his and tugged. "Abby and I need to talk. Have a good night," he said and led her in a swift trot outside.

"That was rude," she sputtered as they stood a few steps outside the back door of the Hitching Post. "He was trying to look after me, which is more than you can say. Besides—"

Cade shut her off when he pressed his mouth against hers. She made an unintelligible sound of protest that turned into a moan, when he changed the tenor of the kiss and slid his tongue past her lips.

Abby sighed and lifted her hand to his shoulders. She pulled back and stared into his eyes. "What the hell were you doing with that woman last night?"

"Exactly what I told you. My dad got sick, so I had to take the interview. The reporter's questions were nonstop. She insisted on dinner. That was when I sent you the text."

"Hmmph," she said, still suspicious. "You could have called me after the interview ended."

"I thought about it, but I figured you might be busy with classwork and I didn't want to interrupt your sleep if you'd hit the sack," he said.

She stared at him silently.

"Why are we arguing when you and I both know we want to go back to my place and be alone?" he asked in a husky voice that touched her in secret places.

"Is that what you want?" she asked.

"It was what I wanted last night," he said.

Her heart tripped over itself. "Then let's go."

She got into his SUV with him, and at every stop sign he reached across the console to kiss her. Their stops grew longer and hotter. At the next-to-last stop, he gave her a long French kiss. It must have been a very long one because a car behind them beeped.

Cade swore under his breath and raced forward. He glanced at her at the next stoplight, but set his jaw as if he were trying to steel himself from kissing her again. Finally, he pulled into his driveway and stopped the car just outside his front porch. He jumped out of the driver's side of the car and rounded the vehicle to open her door. Then he helped her out and rushed her up the steps and inside his house, slamming the door behind them.

Pushing her against the wall, he tangled his fingers through her hair and took her mouth. "Who was that guy back there? Is he important to you?"

"No," she admitted. "He's just been asking me out for a week or so. I've turned him down."

"Except tonight?" he asked, and she could feel the tension in his strong body. The hint of possessiveness in his tone made her feel as if he'd turned her upside down.

She took a deep breath. "How would you have felt if you'd received a text photo of me having dinner with another man when we were supposed to get together?"

She felt him hold his breath then he released it. "I wouldn't have been happy."

"Well, I wasn't, either," she said, meeting his gaze dead-on.

"You didn't have anything to worry about," he told her.

"How was I supposed to know that?" she challenged.

"I'll show you," he said and took her mouth again. They tugged off each other's clothes, and soon enough she felt her naked skin against his. He kissed her and touched her as if he couldn't get enough of her. Abby could hardly breathe with the passion he expressed to her.

As if he could no longer wait, he pulled on protection and took her against the wall. Abby wrapped her legs around his waist and clung to him. It was the most exhilarating experience of her life. She almost couldn't believe it was happening, but then he thrust high inside her, groaning his release.

Abby had never felt so desired and so desirable. She'd dreamed of being with Cade, but the reality was so much more powerful than she'd ever thought possible. A burst of emotion rolled through her, stinging her eyes with its intensity and to her horror, tears began to fall down her face.

Trying to shield her tears from Cade, she turned her head away, praying she'd moved fast enough.

"What's wrong?" he asked, still holding her tightly against him. He slid his hand up to her cheek and felt the telltale wetness. "Did I hurt you?" he asked, sounding horrified.

"No, no," she insisted, swiping at her tears as he lowered her unsteady feet to the floor. "It's ju—just—" She sniffed, damning her emotions. "When I saw that photo of you with her, I thought the other night had been a one-night stand, after all, and—"

"It wasn't," he told her, cradling her against him. "I'm sorry you got that picture. You can check out the feature when it hits the stands. It was really important to the business."

Abby took a deep breath and tried to get herself together. She was appalled that she'd cried.

"I promise," he said, lifting her face to his. "Don't cry anymore. It kills me."

She made herself smile. "No more crying," she promised.

He lifted her up and carried her down the hallway into his bedroom. Placing her gently on his bed, he followed her down. "You are so beautiful," he told her. "You're so much more than I realized."

Her swollen, battered heart eased just a little with his words and she curled into him. "You can skip the condoms," she told him.

"Why?" he asked, looking intently at her.

"I'm on the pill for bad cramps and I'm pretty sure neither one of us has a social disease," she said.

He groaned in anticipation of pleasure. "You just made my day even better," he told her and began to make love to her again.

Two hours later, she pulled on one of his shirts and joined him in the kitchen. "Let me fix you some scrambled eggs and toast," he said. "I'd like to offer you more, but I'm running low on groceries because it's our busy season."

"I don't need any—"

"You're not hungry?" he asked. "Because I'm starving."

Now that he mentioned it, she pressed her hand to her stomach. "Scrambled eggs sound good."

He pulled bread from the freezer and popped four slices into the toaster while he turned on the gas stove. She watched him, naked from the waist up, as he cracked eggs into a bowl and beat them silly. After pouring a little oil in the skillet, he tossed in the eggs and stirred them. Minutes later, both the toast and eggs were ready.

Cade put the food on plates and nudged her to the table. "There," he said, setting a plate in front of her. "I'll have something better for you next time. And there will be a next time," he said, meeting her gaze as he bit off a piece of toast.

Abby took a tentative bite of eggs, surprised to find them cooked perfectly.

"What? You don't like the eggs?" he asked.

"Actually you did a great job with them, not over-cooked, not undercooked."

"You sound surprised," he said.

"Well, you're a bachelor carpenter. You haven't men-tioned taking cooking classes," she said and scooped another mouthful.

"You thought I was completely useless in the kitchen?"

"I didn't say that," she said. "I just didn't think it was your forte," she said. "Delicious. You didn't even burn the toast."

He chuckled. "That's because it was frozen. You can probably cook circles around me, but I can fix a few things worth eating. Steak, barbecued chicken, fish on the grill."

She smiled. "If it involves fire, you're there. Right?" she asked.

He met her gaze and grinned. "Stop looking at me and finish your eggs before they get cold."

Abby bit her lip and looked at him, anyway.

He looked at her and his gaze held an irresistible mix of sensuality and Cade. "I mean it, Abby. Stop looking at me or I'm going to haul you off to my bed again."

"Would that be such a bad thing?" she asked.

He shook his head and scrubbed his hand over his face. "Finish your eggs. I don't want to be responsible for making you faint."

"Then you should have put on a shirt," she told him and ate her eggs.

Although they got a little distracted, Cade managed to help her get dressed and he bundled her up and led her to his car. "I don't want you having to answer a lot of questions about where you've been," he said and he drove toward her parents' house.

"I don't mind if people know you and I are seeing each other," she said. "Do you?"

"I don't like people poking into my business. I don't want either of us to have to deal with gossips. I just want us to be for us right now," he said and covered her hand with his. "Is that okay with you?"

Warmth flooded her. When he looked at her that way, she would say yes to anything he asked. Plus he made an important point. Even though she had known Cade forever, they hadn't shared an adult relationship very long. After what Laila had said to her the other night, Abby didn't want to hear the opinions of any detractors. She was glad Cade felt the same way.

He stopped in front of her house and pulled her against him once more. "You feel so good it's hard to let you go," he said.

Her heart skipped over itself at his words, and she sighed. "That makes two of us."

"It's supposed to be unseasonably warm for the next day or two. If the weather matches up with the forecast and you're caught up on your classes, maybe I could take you for a spin on my Harley."

"I'd love that," she said, remembering how envious she'd felt all those times Laila had ridden off with Cade on his motorcycle.

"You'll still need to dress warm," he warned her.

"Call me," she said, knowing she would be pulling a late night for her classes in order to make time for a ride with Cade. It would be worth it, she told herself. She could sleep some other time.

The following afternoon, Abby drove out to Cade's house to meet him for their motorcycle ride. The temps were supposed hit the mid-fifties. For Montana in the winter, that was considered a heat wave. She was so excited she felt like a kid at Christmas. He approved her warm clothing. "Good job with the ski mask and gloves. Just hang on and lean with my body on the curves," he said and put a helmet on her head.

She mounted his prized Harley behind him and wrapped her arms around him as he started the engine. "You ready?" he asked.

"I was born ready for this," she said.

He laughed and they were off. Cade steered the motorcycle toward the countryside. Although the roads were perfectly dry, some stubborn snow packs remained here and there. Abby knew this jump in temperature was just a tease. They would get snow again before the week was done. That knowledge made her all the more determined to enjoy the ride.

The moutains loomed with dramatic beauty over the plains, providing breathtaking vistas. A half hour later, Cade pulled into a small diner and parked the Harley near the door. He helped her off the motorcycle and Abby pulled off her helmet and ski mask. She was surprised to feel a little wobbly.

Cade must have noticed because he laughed as he steadied her. "Still feel like you're riding?" he asked.

She nodded. "I can still hear the buzz in my ears, too."

"You'll get used to it," he said. "You just need some practice. I figured we could grab a bite to eat here. If you're not hungry, they make good coffee and hot chocolate."

"Yes to the second," she said and shook her hair as they walked inside. "I bet my hair looks crazy," she said, raking her hands through it self-consciously, feeling it crackle with electricity.

He sat across from her in a booth and shook his head.

"You look beautiful. Your cheeks and lips are red and you hair reminds me of what it looks like after we—" He broke off as a waitress approached them.

"How ya doin', Cade?" the thirtysomething red-haired waitress asked with a wink and a smile. "It's been a while, but I guess you don't ride that Harley through a blizzard."

"It's true, Dani. I'll take a club sandwich and coffee. What about you, Abby?" he asked.

"Hot chocolate," she said.

"You sure like 'em young these days, don't you? Are you sure she's legal?" Dani asked with another wink.

Slightly irritated by the waitress's remark, Abby smiled. "I look younger than I am. Must be all that clean living. I guess I need to dirty up my lifestyle a little so I can catch up," she joked.

"No need for that," Cade countered.

The waitress laughed. "I like her sense of humor. Got a little kick behind that sweet face. Good for you. I'll get your coffee and hot chocolate," she said and walked away.

"You handled her pretty well," he said. "Dani's known for ribbing people."

"I have a feeling she's trying to get your attention. She looked at you like she wanted to gobble you up. I guess I can't blame her," she said with an exaggerated sigh.

He chuckled at her. "You keep surprising me. I just never would have expected sweet little Abby to have a wild bone in her body."

"I'm pretty sure I have more than one. I just haven't discovered all of them yet," she said.

He groaned. "Heaven help me. What do you think of the ride so far?"

Dani delivered their beverages and scooted to another table.

"It's glorious," she said. "We are spoiled with all these beautiful views and I think we see them so much we stop really looking at them. You can't avoid it when you're on the motorcycle. The mountains and hills and lakes are right there in your face."

"That's one of the things I like about riding. Nothing between me and nature," he said. "Did you get too cold?"

"No," she said, taking a sip of her hot chocolate. "You kept me warm."

His eyes darkened in sexual awareness. "You're asking for trouble again," he said. "Do you say these kinds of things to other men?"

"No. Why would I do that when it's you I want?"

Cade felt the need ripple through him at the look in her eyes. It was amazing how such an innocent girl— woman, he mentally corrected himself—could get him stirred up with just a side comment or the way she looked at him. Even the way she sipped her hot chocolate was sexy to him. Abby Cates was looking like a lot of trouble, but he didn't feel like running the other way. At least, not yet.

After he talked her into sharing a few bites of his club sandwich, they hit the road again. He slowed as they drew close to Silver Stallion Lake. The lake served as a recreation area for local families and visitors. He'd spent a few summers lifeguarding during the summers.

He pulled to a stop and cut the engine. "I have a lot of memories from here."

"Me, too. It was the first time you held me in your arms," she said.

He swung his head to look at her and pulled off his helmet. "What?"

"Yes," she said, pulling off her own helmet and the ski mask. She had an impish gleam in her eyes. "You were giving swimming lessons. Some water went down the wrong way and you rescued me," she said in a melo-dramatic tone.

Cade rolled his eyes.

"You don't remember?"

"I can't say I do," he said, racking his brain. "In my defense, I pulled a lot of choking kids out of the water. How old were you?" he asked, then shook his head and lifted his hand. "Don't tell me."

She laughed and swatted at his shoulder. "Feeling old?"

He thought of everything that had happened in his life since those carefree summers at Silver Stallion Lake and the truth was he did feel old. Between the loss of his mother and Dominique, and his work at the shop, he'd felt gutted and empty more often than not.

"You're not old, Cade. You just need to get out and have a little more fun," Abby said. "I can help with that," she offered in that sexy voice that made his blood heat. She squeezed her arms around him and he felt a surprising corresponding squeeze on the inside, somewhere near his heart.

"I might just take you up on it," he said and started the engine. "Get your helmet on," he said and followed his own advice. He accelerated, leaving the lake behind him, but he longed for that lighthearted young man he'd once been.

Abby sat on Cade's sofa wrapped in his arms. A fire blazed in the fireplace and they both sipped hot cider. She couldn't imagine anything better. She leaned her head against Cade's chest and stroked his hand. After several more moments passed, it occurred to her that Cade hadn't spoken for quite awhile.

"You're quiet," she said. "What are you thinking about?"

He sighed. "Nothing," he said. "Lots of stuff."

She smiled at his response. "I think I'll go with your second answer. What kind of stuff?"

"Oh, what things were like before my mother died. How quickly it all changed. My father changed overnight. My younger brothers went a little wild. I considered it, but I saw how much my dad was hurting. I didn't want to add to the pain. My sister, Holly, she just seemed lost. Dad doted on her, but for a while, there, he was a dead man walking."

"I know that was hard for you," she said.

He nodded. "It was," he said. "And the holidays were the worst. My mother was the one to make holidays happen, so when she was gone, we didn't know what to do. The holidays would hit and we didn't plan for them, so we would fumble around and throw something together." He chuckled. "I can't tell you how many cooking disasters we had. Lesson number one, you need to thaw the turkey."

Abby stroked his hand and studied his face. "Well, at least that's a funny memory."

His smile faded. "Yeah. One of the few."

"I bet there were some other funny ones," she said.

Cade nodded. "The gifts we bought. One of my brothers bought Holly bubble bath that made her break out. My father gave us savings bonds and stale chocolate my mother had bought a long time ago. He forgot to buy the new stuff, so he gave us the old chocolate. We all ate it, wanting to feel like we had when we were younger, when she was alive, but it didn't work."

"I'm sorry," she said. "I'm sorry she died."

"Yeah, I am, too. And then there was…Dominique," he said.

Abby's stomach clenched. She'd heard very little about Dominique, the woman who had stolen Cade's heart. Her family had lived in town briefly and she'd attended the same local university as Abby. Abby had heard Dominique had been a one-of-a-kind dark-haired beauty. A lot of guys had chased her, but she'd liked Cade best.

"You were serious about her," Abby said.

He nodded.

"Everyone said you were going to propose to her

when she returned from her trip to California," she added.

"Everyone was right about that," he said. "She took off between Christmas and New Year's to meet some friends in California. I figured I would surprise her when she got back. I'd bought the ring."

As much as she wanted Cade for herself, the thought of his loss stabbed deeply at her. "I can't imagine how horrible that must have been."

"Pretty damn bad," he said. "And her parents partly blamed me because I didn't propose before she left. They were convinced she would have never gone if I'd asked her first."

Her breath stopped in her chest. "They blamed you? That's horrible."

He shrugged. "Maybe they were right. I wanted her to have a break. She'd been working hard at school. She was looking forward to the beach."

Abby shook her head. "It's just wrong. You were being sweet and—" It was hard for her to say the words, but she swallowed back her own pain. "And loving. Couldn't they see how hurt you were?"

"They were devastated. They couldn't see past their own pain," he said. "I can't blame them."

"So all of this is why the holidays suck for you," she said.

He paused a moment then nodded. "Yeah, I guess so."

Abby took a deep breath and slid her hand to Cade's jaw. "I would if I could, but I can't bring back Dominique or your mom. I can't make things the way they were, but if you're open to it, I can probably make things happier than they have been."

He lifted an eyebrow at her. "You think?"

"Only if you're open to it. If you're not open, I can't do anything. I'm no Houdini."

His lips twitched. "And if I'm open?" he asked, lifting his hand to push a strand of hair from her face.

"I'll surprise you," she said.

"You've already done that."

"Well, I'll do it again."

Chapter Eight

The following night, Cade arrived home and was surprised to find a Christmas wreath hanging from his front door. *What the—* He opened his front door and smelled the delicious scent of something he definitely had not cooked. His dog greeted him with a wagging tale and anticipation of a few bites of whatever was cooking.

"I love you, darlin'," he said, rubbing her soft, furry head. "But the vet says you should only get dry dog food. And this smells so good I may not be able to share."

Cade walked farther into the house, noticing the sound of his television playing the sweet music of Monday-night football. "Hello? I hope you're not an ax murderer, but if you are, can I eat before you kill me?"

Abby poked her head from the kitchen doorway and smiled. "No plans to kill you," she said. "Unless you complain it's overcooked. Have you looked at the time?"

"You need to remember I had to make up for all the time I lost doing that stupid interview instead of my real work," he complained.

"Yeah, eating a meal at the Hitching Post with a pretty woman making eyes all over you," she said. "Pure agony."

"I guess I shouldn't have brought that up."

"I guess you shouldn't have," she said. "But we could change stations if you're interested in some beef stew."

"Do I have to beg?"

She gave a slow smile. "That's a tempting image," she said. "But I think I'll save it for another time. Come on and I'll pour a bowl. I have biscuits, too."

Cade's mouth drooled. He tried to remember the last time he'd had homemade biscuits and couldn't. Striding into the kitchen with the dog at his heels, he blinked at a turkey decoration, this one hanging from one of his kitchen lights.

"That's something," he said, pointing at the bird.

"Pull his foot," she said, arranging biscuits on a small plate.

Curious, Cade pulled it. Nothing happened.

"Other foot," she said as she placed his meal on the table.

Cade pulled the other foot and the turkey gave a *gobble-gobble* sound. Cade stared at the stuffed bird and couldn't resist pulling the leg again. The turkey gave another *gobble-gobble*.

"I don't know what to say," he said, tempted to pull the foot again, but the aroma of the beef stew called to him at a cellular level. He sat down at the table. "Where the hell did you find it?"

"Addictive, isn't it?" she said with a lone biscuit in front of her. "Seems silly, but it's hard to resist pulling the turkey's foot."

"Is that all you're going to eat?" he asked, his spoon poised over the stew.

She gave a gentle, crocodile smile. "I ate hours ago."

He growled then took his first bite. "Food of the gods," he said. "Who fixed this? Your Mom?"

Quicker than he could take his next breath, she pulled his bowl away from him and he realized he'd made a huge mistake. "Because you're too busy to cook. You have a wicked-crazy schedule. No time for cooking something this amazing." He paused. "Is this when I beg?"

She slid the bowl back in front of him. "Your habit of underestimating me is getting a little old. Even old Mr. Henson tried to tell you I was a good cook."

"You're right," he said, taking another bite and swallowing a moan of pleasure and satisfaction. Cade was a bachelor, all too familiar with frozen dinners and restaurant meals. A home-cooked meal was a thing of wonder to him. "I will never underestimate your cooking again."

"That's good to know," she said, as she leaned her

chin on her palms and watched. "Is that the only way you won't underestimate me?"

Cade thought of how she'd made love to him and desire thudded through him. "No, but I won't finish this meal if you keep reminding me."

She smiled. "So, are you rooting for the Eagles?"

He met her gaze and felt his heart lift at her effort to let him enjoy the meal she'd prepared for him. It occurred to Cade that with the exception of that turkey hanging from the light in the kitchen, he could get used to Abby greeting him with a hot meal and a welcoming smile. Tension eased out of him. She kept surprising him, and he wasn't inclined to ask her to stop.

After he finished his second bowl, he built a fire and they watched the game. In a manner of speaking, anyway. Cade couldn't tell you the score at halftime because he'd been too busy taking off Abby's clothes and making love to her. He pulled her on top of him and she rode him, bringing herself and him to climax. He watched her smooth, creamy skin shimmering in the firelight. Her face glowed with arousal. The expression in her eyes called to him. At the same time, it frightened the hell out of him.

A half hour later, he cradled her in his arms.

"I should head home soon," she said. "It's getting late."

"It would be nice if you could stay all night," he said, brushing his mouth over her soft jaw.

She gave a soft sound of pleasure. "It could be arranged, but it would take some planning."

"Oh, really," he said. "How's that?"

"I've pulled all-nighters with study groups before. I've gone out of town on girl trips."

"If you stayed overnight with me, you wouldn't be studying schoolwork, I can promise you that," he growled.

She laughed. "No, I would just say something along those lines to my parents."

"I don't like the idea of you lying to your family about me," he said.

"Well, you want to keep it on the down low. And I'd just as soon not get grilled about it, either." She sighed. "Maybe I can figure something out. But I should head out now."

"See you tomorrow night?" he asked reluctantly, standing with her, pulling on his jeans as she got dressed.

"No. Tomorrow night I'm with my ROOTS girls. During the day, I'm helping with the community-center Thanksgiving production. Thank goodness, they'll be giving their performance soon. Then they'll be out on break. That reminds me, I should stop by and check on Mr. Henson, too." She glanced up at Cade. "So tomorrow I'll be slammed. Do you want to try for lunch on Wednesday or is that too public for you?"

"I can do lunch on Wednesday," he said, but was surprised at his eagerness to spend more time with her. Maybe it was the sex. Lord, he hoped so because a big part of him wanted to occupy all of her free time.

"You'll have to keep your hands off of me," she

warned him with a sexy tilt of her lips. "You'll have to pretend we're just friends. Are you sure you can do that?"

With the way she was looking at him, he suspected it might be more difficult than he would have expected, but Cade had a long history with self-restraint. "I guess I'll just have to buck up and do my best," he said, pulling her back into his arms. "We'll make up for it some other time."

Cade insisted on following her home. It didn't feel right to have her drive home by herself. If they'd been officially dating, he would have always walked her to her door. As she got out of her car, she waved at him and walked into her family home.

Cade stared after her. She was so young, tender and sweet. He knew she was stronger than he'd originally thought, far more of a woman, but he still feared that he would hurt her. He couldn't help believing that eventually Abby would want all of him, and Cade had lost part of himself a long time ago, and that part would never come back.

Abby helped at the community center and spent the afternoon in class. Afterward, she squeezed in some time at the university library. Since she'd been spending so much time with Cade, she was really having to maximize her study time. Sipping a bottle of water, she made notes for yet another paper she was writing.

"One of your friends told me I might find you here," a male voice said.

Abby glanced up to find Daniel looking down at her with a smile. "Uh, hi," she said, completely surprised. "Who—"

"Char," he said and sat down next to her. "You disappeared the other night at the Hitching Post. I was concerned about you. That guy looked pretty intense."

"Cade?" she said. "Cade would never hurt me. No, I've been crazy busy and I can't talk now because I need to work on this paper."

"Rain check?" he asked and, when she paused, he covered her hand with his. "You gotta give me a rain check after I tracked you down."

Uncomfortable, she moved her hand away from his. "You really shouldn't have."

"I see a woman who makes me curious and I gotta find out more," he said. "But I can wait. Take care. I'll keep in touch," he said and strolled out of the library.

Abby frowned after him. She would definitely need to speak to Char about passing any further personal information on to this guy. The more often she saw him, the more uncomfortable he made her and he didn't seem the least bit discouraged. She shrugged off her uneasiness and refocused on her paper, wondering what Carl Jung would have to say about Daniel.

A half hour before her meeting with the ROOTS girls, Abby left the library and grabbed a fast-food burger and soda. She usually skipped caffeine this late in the day, but she could feel herself starting to fade. From her first visit at ROOTS, Abby had learned she had to be on her toes with the girls.

The group started out small and quiet, so she helped the girls with their homework. Since many of the girls came from such disrupted homes, it was often difficult for them to find a quiet place to concentrate. Thirty minutes into their meeting time Katrina and Keisha burst into the room.

"You have to report him. You have to. What if it gets worse?" Keisha asked Katrina.

"Shut up," Katrina hissed. "If I ignore him, he'll go away."

Abby stood, alarmed at the bruises she saw on Katrina's face. "Girls," she said.

Keisha looked at Abby and lifted her chin defiantly. "You talk to her. She won't listen to me."

"Katrina?" she said. "Would you like some water or hot chocolate? We can talk over there if you like," she said.

Katrina was a sixteen-year-old with bleached blond hair who did her best to make herself look tough with the black leather and kohl eyeliner she wore. Abby knew that beneath her tough exterior, the girl had a mother who was rarely at home and Katrina was struggling to stay away from a bad crowd at school. She'd been suspended for smoking in the girls' room.

"It's no big deal," Katrina said as she swiped her damp face with the back of her hand. "It's my mother's new boyfriend. He's been staying over and he gets pissed when I spend too much time in the bathroom. I'll just spend the night with one of my friends. He'll cool down."

Abby didn't like the sound of this at all. She handed Katrina a cup of hot chocolate. "Does your mother know?"

Katrina shrugged, but her hand was shaking as she held the cup. "She's too busy. She's working three jobs. He says he was laid off," she said, but her tone suggested she didn't believe him.

"How long has he been around?" Abby asked.

"A couple months. He was okay in the beginning, but once he started staying overnight, he thought he could tell me what to do when my mom wasn't around. He really likes his whiskey. Seems like he drinks a bottle every day."

"I'm so sorry you've had to go through this," Abby said.

"Don't feel sorry for me. I can take care of myself."

Abby nodded. "If Keisha was in this situation, what advice would you give her?"

Katrina gave a short laugh that almost sounded like a sob. "Keisha wouldn't be in this situation. She would kick his butt out of the house."

"Okay. What about Shannon?"

Katrina paused. "Shannon's different."

"What would you tell her?"

"As much as it sucks, I would tell her to rat on him. It's such a pain to deal with child protective services. If only we were eighteen," she said. "Everything would be easier."

"Not so much," Abby said. "But that's not the point. I want you to give an official report. I could do it, but

I want you to care enough about yourself to do it for yourself."

Katrina sighed. "I'll have to stay with some super strict people I don't know," she said.

"Maybe not," Abby said. "Plus it wouldn't be forever. Do you really think your mother would keep this guy around if she knew he was hitting you?"

Katrina shrugged. "She doesn't want to deal with it."

"Which means you have to," Abby said. "You deserve to live in a situation where you are not abused and neglected. If I've helped you learn anything, you've learned that."

"I don't want to be with people who are always telling me what to do. You know I'm not used to that," she said.

"It's temporary," Abby said. "That's what you have to remember. You're a strong young woman and this is one of those times when you need to be your own best friend. I'll go with you to make the report."

Katrina swore under her breath. "You really think I have to do it?"

"You've been around here long enough to see what happened with other girls in this situation. You are a very smart, very capable young woman. I think if you end up with someone who wants to know where you are and when it may not be fun, but it will be a lot better than worrying about whether you'll be beaten. And I repeat, it won't be forever."

Katrina sighed. "Okay, okay. Can we do it now? Believe it or not, I don't want to miss school tomorrow. I have an exam."

"Let me take a few more minutes with the other girls, then you and I can head out," she said.

Abby talked to the other girls while Keisha walked over to give Katrina a big hug and shook her finger at the girl. Abby felt a surge of warmth at how the girls were supporting each other.

Hours later, Katrina was safely tucked in bed at her temporary foster parents' home while her mother's boyfriend was brought in for questioning and would soon be charged with assault on a minor. Before that, the drama had intensified: Katrina's mother arrived in a sad state, apologizing profusely to her daughter and promising to do a better job.

Although it was nearly 2:00 a.m. when Abby arrived home, she felt a sense of temporary relief that she knew Katrina was safe, and she was so proud of her ROOTS girl for choosing to stick up for herself. These girls came across as tough, but many of them had been abused, and one of Abby's biggest goals had been to help them grow away from a victim mentality.

Abby said a little prayer, and just before she drifted off to sleep, she thought of Cade. She wished all of those girls at ROOTS could find a man as strong and gentle as Cade.

Cade met Abby at DJ's for lunch on Wednesday. He arrived a couple minutes early and ordered coffee for himself. He didn't mention that anyone would be joining him, but sat in one of the booths at the back of the restaurant. He saw her open the door and glance around, pushing her hair behind her ear. Instead of waving, he simply stood, and within an eye blink, she saw him and moved toward him.

"What a surprise to see you here," she said in a mocking voice and gave him a far-too-quick hug before she sat down. "Nice to see you," she said.

He drank in the sight of her, noticing the dark circles under her eyes and the slight pallor of her skin. "Did you sleep at all last night?"

"Why?" she asked. "Do I look like a hag?"

"I would never call you a hag," he said.

"Well, something must have made you say that," she said.

The waitress showed up then. "Lunch ribs with coleslaw for me," he said. "What about you?" he asked Abby.

She gave a quick glance at the menu and shrugged. "Barbecue sandwich and fries. I need some grease."

"And to drink?" the waitress asked.

"A chocolate milk shake," she said.

The waitress smiled. "Excellent choice. I'll be back soon."

"So I look like a hag," she said to Cade.

"I did *not* say that. You just look very tired. Circles under your eyes, your skin is pale—"

"I need to get better with concealer. I think it's a required skill. Think about it. If you can hide dark circles, then no one will know that you spent the last night with a girl who'd been beat up by her mother's boyfriend."

"Oh, my God. Who's the girl?" Cade asked. "Who's the guy? If you want me to talk to him—"

She finally smiled, and it was like the sun broke through. "I knew you'd say something like that. That's one of the reasons I—" She broke off. "One of the reasons I like you."

Warmth spread throughout his chest, but he tried to shrug it off. "Is the girl okay?"

"For now," Abby said. "I had to talk her into reporting the incident and the guy. I stayed with her thoughout the whole experience and the poor girl was put through the ringer. The temporary foster parents seem pretty nice if they can deal with her independence. She's used to doing everything for herself, which means she's not used to taking orders or filling anyone in on her whereabouts."

"That's a rough way to live," he said. "You do a good job with those kids at ROOTS."

"Sometimes I wonder if they do more for me. But I have to tell you when someone has been physically abused, it really draws the line about what needs to be done. Her sweet face was bruised all over. I was just glad I could be a tiny part of getting her to a safe place."

"I bet you're a much bigger part than you think you are," he said, wishing he could take her hands in his, pull her against him so she could relax for a little while.

She shrugged. "What's important is that Katrina is safe. I hope things will continue to be on the upswing for her. I'll be watching, that's for sure."

"Hmm," he said.

She shot him a sideways glance. "What does that mean?"

"It means you're always talking about me having a hero complex. I'm starting to wonder if you don't have the same problem," he said.

Her lips tilted again. "Very funny," she said.

"I'm not being funny," he said.

"Sure you are," she said and the waitress delivered their food. "Thanks," she said to the woman.

"My pleasure," she said. "You two let me know if you need anything else, okay?"

Both of them dug in to their food, creating a comfortable silence. Abby took a few sips of her milk shake. "Brain freeze," she said, squeezing the bridge of her nose then shaking her head. "How have things been at work? Any more gorgeous reporters?"

"No more reporters at all. It's back to me and the wood. Sometimes I make art. Sometimes I make furniture. I do a lot of knocking, sawing and sanding, but no one needs to call the police because of it, thank goodness."

"That's a funny thought," she said. "You sawing on a piece of wood and a bunch of wood specialists come in and arrest you."

"Very funny," he said, clearly disagreeing with her. "But the truth is it's pretty satisfying. I'm sure it's not as big as having a kid, but it's been good for me. You really look like you could use a nap. If I were in charge, I would take you off to bed so you could get some rest."

"I'll survive. I'm a young college student. We exist on adrenaline, right?"

"If you say so," he said. "I'd still like to drag you off and make you take a nap."

She paused a half beat, studying him. "I may not wake up for a long time if you did that, and today, I've still got a long ways to go."

"Don't burn the candle at both ends too long. Mother Nature has a way of kicking you on your butt if you push her too far."

"Sounds like you're speaking from experience," she said and swallowed more of her shake.

"Unfortunately," he said in a wry voice.

The waitress delivered the check and when Abby glanced up, Cade noticed she cringed and sorta hunched down. As soon as the waitress left, he studied her. "What's up?"

She lifted one shoulder, glanced over it then looked back at Cade. "Probably nothing. It just seems like this guy keeps showing up everywhere I am. It's like he has a GPS on me or something."

His sense of protectiveness shot up inside him. "Who is he?"

"He's a server at the Hitching Post. He was flirting with my friends and me the night I was out with them, but I wasn't all that impressed. I think he's one of those guys who is attracted to a girl because she's not interested. I think he sees it as a challenge."

"What's his name?"

Abby lifted her gaze as if she were searching her brain. "Um. *D* something. Daniel."

"Daniel what?"

She shook her head. "I have no idea."

"Is he the guy who was hitting on you the other night? Do you think he's stalking you?" he asked, his gut tightening. He didn't like the idea of anyone bothering Abby.

She paused a half beat and shook her head again. "No, he can't be. It's just that he showed up at the university library and he doesn't even go there, so that creeped me out a little. It's probably nothing. I'm probably freaking out because I need sleep," she joked. "Don't worry."

But he would. If he didn't worry, he would think about it. "Let me know if he pops up anywhere else during the next few days."

"It's really nothing," she said.

"Then it won't be a big deal for you to tell me if he shows up," he said. "Deal?"

Her lips lifted in a slow smile. "Deal." She took another sip of her milk shake through the straw and gave a quick, soft sound of approval that reminded him of... *No need thinking about that,* he told himself.

"Where are you headed? I'll walk you to your car," he said.

"Are you sure you want to do that? People may talk," she said, her eyes glinting with flirty challenge.

"I'll keep my hands to myself," he said, barely containing a growl.

"Well, darn," Abby said and stood, and Cade was treated to the sight of the sexy sashay of her sweet, round bottom as they walked from DJ's.

Friday couldn't come soon enough, Abby thought as she sat in the diner waiting to meet two classmates to discuss their presentation for class the following Tuesday. In charge of the Jung presentation, she filled out a few more note cards as she waited.

"You never stop, do you?"

Abby's stomach knotted at the voice that was becoming all too familiar. She reluctantly glanced up. "Daniel. What a surprise," she said.

He smiled. "It's not that big of a surprise. I know you like this place and you frequent it at night. You know I'd like us to spend more time together."

His smile was a little too practiced. It bothered her. "I hate to be blunt, but us spending more time together? It's not going to happen."

"Sure it is. You'll catch a break soon, be ready for some entertainment." He bent his knees and braced himself on the table so his face was level with hers. "I'm more than ready to provide it."

"No," she said, wishing she didn't have to be even more blunt. It was as if he'd completely forgotten the other time she'd turned him down. "You don't understand. I'm not interested in having a relationship with you."

He shrugged. "No problem. We can start out having fun."

Abby was tempted to scream, but she swallowed the urge. "You know how there are girls who say no and mean yes?" she asked. "I'm not one of those girls."

Chapter Nine

"I'm on my way," she said after Cade picked up his cell phone. "Can we have some sort of fabulous take-out for dinner?"

"Such as?" Cade asked.

"Lobster, filet mignon, asparagus, au gratin potatoes, chocolate mousse, followed by some time in a hot tub and maybe one of those martinis you got me at the Hitching Post. Nothing too complicated," she said.

He chuckled. "Right."

"Pizza and soda. I hardly ever drink soda, but tonight I want to be bad."

He laughed louder. "If soda is your version of bad..." he began.

"Don't mock me. At least I kept it simple."

"I'll see what I can do," he said. " Stella will be glad to see you when you get here."

"Anyone else around there who'll be happy to see me?" she asked.

"Me," he said.

Twenty minutes later, she pulled into Cade's driveway, stopping as she drew close to his porch. Normally, she would jump out of her car and bound up the steps, but she was seriously dragging tonight. She hoped she didn't embarrass herself by falling asleep unexpectedly. It didn't help that just as she left the community center this morning, Daniel had been waiting in front of the building. She hadn't said anything to her friends yet, but she thought she was going to have to have a conversation with Char. Her friend probably was just trying to nudge her into giving in to a fun time with a hot guy. Char had no idea that Abby was involved with someone else.

Frustration nicked at her. In one way, she chafed at the idea of keeping her relationship with Cade secret. In another way, she agreed with him that she didn't want to endure anyone else's thoughts or assessments of her and Cade. So, for now, she just had to be evasive. Not her best talent.

Sighing, Abby got out of her car and stretched. The wind whipped over her, reminding her that it was still winter. The warm day last weekend had been a quick little treat and it was gone now. Bundling her collar upward, she climbed the stairs and knocked on the door.

Stella barked, and within seconds Cade opened the

door. "Well, look what the wind blew in. Very nice," he said, tugging her inside and pressing his mouth against hers. "You're cold," he said.

"That's why I mentioned a hot tub," she said and glanced behind him. "You have one in your back pocket?"

"Very cute," he said. "I don't have a hot tub, but I have a tub filled with hot water. If you're interested," he said.

She stared at him in disbelief. "Really? A tub? For me? A bath? Omigosh, I can't believe it. An early Christmas gift."

"It's just a tub," he warned, guiding her toward the hall bathroom.

"Haven't you noticed how many sisters I have? Do you know how often I get to take a bath? Take a guess," she said, staring at the steaming water. It was all she could do not to instantly strip and jump in the tub.

"Not often. Go ahead. Get in. Just don't drown," he said.

She smiled and squeezed his arm. "Oh, I won't drown. I had an excellent swimming teacher."

He shook his head. "Shut up and take a bath."

"Really? Are you sure I don't need to wait for the pizza?" she asked.

He shook his head again. "No need," he said. "But don't fall asleep."

Abby shut the door behind him, stripped out of her clothes, twisted her hair into a knot on top of her head and put her foot in the steaming water. It was *hot*.

Which made it perfect. She eased the rest of her body inside the tub and leaned her head against the back of the tub. Abby was in heaven. Her long showers rarely lasted over eight minutes, so soaking in Cade's bathtub felt like the most indulgent luxury possible.

She felt the muscles in her body relax, tendon by tendon. From some point in her brain, she thought she heard Cade's doorbell ring. Pizza? she wondered, but couldn't find it in herself to move more than a millimeter. Had her bones turned to butter? She hadn't felt this relaxed in…how many years?

Mentally playing a jazz song, she closed her eyes and just floated.

Seconds later, she heard Cade knocking on the door and instantly sat up, startled. "What?" she asked, wondering when the water had turned cold. She shivered at the temperature. It had been so lovely and hot, like, two minutes ago.

"Abby, I'm starting to get worried. Answer me. Are you conscious?" Cade asked from the other side of the door.

"I'm here. I'm awake." Beginning to shiver, she stepped out of the tub. "Is the pizza here?"

"In a manner of speaking," Cade said, opening the door and extending a terry-cloth robe in her direction. "You want this?"

"That would be perfect," she said, grabbing the robe and clutching it against her.

"Don't drag your feet. I don't want the pizza to get cold," he said.

"Okay, okay," she said to herself then spoke louder as she towel dried herself. "I'll be out in a minute."

She pushed her hands through the sleeves of the robe, tied the sash and bent over to pull the plug out of the drain of the tub.

Stepping out of the bathroom, she headed down the hall to the kitchen and found a table spread with steaks, shrimp, baked potatoes, *asparagus*—she noted in shock—and bread. She looked at Cade in surprise. "I thought we were having pizza," she said.

"You don't want it?" he said.

"No," she said. "Of course I do. I'm just so—" She was both amazed and touched. "How did you do this?"

"A little help from my brother. I couldn't pull off the lobster. This time," he added, rubbing his chin thoughtfully.

Unable to stop herself, she threw herself against him and wrapped her arms around him. "I can't believe this. Aren't you Mr. Hotshot?"

He squeezed her against him. "You get this excited about a nice meal?"

"It's not the meal. It's the fact that you would go to trouble to make me happy," she said. As soon as the words were out, she feared she should have kept them in.

"It wasn't that much trouble," he insisted, clearly uncomfortable.

"It was nice. Very nice," she said. "Thank you."

She lifted her lips upward, and he paused a half beat,

then kissed her. The pause bothered her, but then he kissed the bother out of her.

Cade pulled back. "I can't let you distract us from eating this meal."

"Even if I tried my very best?" she said, sliding her fingers down the neck of the robe to the belt.

"Stop," he said. "Or Stella will get this while I'm hauling you off to my bed."

He pulled out a chair for her and she took the seat, reveling in his attention. Abby and Cade ate the steak and vegetables, nibbled on the bread. She sipped a fruity martini he'd concocted for her and poured into a beer mug. "This is fabulous. I haven't had a meal like this in—" She broke off. "I can't remember when I had a meal like this."

"I'm glad you asked for it," he said, nodding. "I should do this more often."

"I didn't ask for it," she said. "I was joking. I told you I was joking. I never expected you to actually to do this."

"So I surprised you?" he asked, a wicked glint in his eyes.

"Yes, you surprised me," she said. "And it's all wonderful, but I'm so full I don't think I can eat one more bite."

"Better make some room," he said, taking another bite of his steak. "There's something chocolate in the fridge."

Surprised again, she shook her head. "You're joking."

"Not me. I guess I can let you take a little break if you need to. Want to sit in front of the fire?"

"As long as you promise to keep me awake," she said.

"Burning the candle at both ends again," he said. "I warned you about that."

"It's temporary. My schedule should ease up soon. Besides, I have to ask you, what time do you get up and go into the shop?"

"That's different," he said. "I'm used to getting up at 5:00 a.m. I've been doing it since…" He shot her a dead-serious look. "Since you were ten."

"You are wicked and horrible. People don't know," she said. "They all think you're this super amazing, wonderful upstanding citizen, but I know the truth."

"And what is the truth?" he asked, his eyes glinting with the devil again.

"You are quite simply the devil," she said. *And I'm falling out of my crush on you and into love with you.* She bit her tongue to keep from saying the words. She'd always known she had a crush on Cade. In her more melodramatic moments, she'd insisted it was a lifelong passion. But real forever love? Oh, no, this wasn't good.

Cade's hand shot out to grip her arm. "Are you okay, Abby? You look a little squeamish. Did the food bother you?"

Abby shook her head. "Not at all. It was wonderful, and you know it. Thank you for arranging such a fabulous meal. I'm very touched," she said, feeling her throat grow swollen with emotion. Oh, heaven help her, she couldn't cry. "I'm also very full, so I'd like to take you up on that offer to sit in front of the fire." She stood. "Let me help you clear the table first."

Moments later, he linked his hand through hers as they walked into his den. It was Friday night, so there wasn't much on television. Abby sank onto the sofa. "Oh, what a day and now what a wonderful night."

"Rough day?" he asked.

"Just busy. Went to the community center, visited Katrina, took an exam and got fitted for a bridesmaid dress." She winced when she realized what she'd said. "I'm sorry. Really sorry."

"It's okay," he said. "I'm happy for Laila."

She searched his gaze and saw that he was telling the truth. A sliver of ease slipped through her and she sighed. "That is really good."

He nodded and pulled her against him. "Anything else?"

"Not really. My car is working great. I'm not behind on my papers. I have a group presentation next week, and I'm ready for my part." She paused. "Um, I guess I should tell you this. I don't have to stay tonight, but I told my mom I might be staying overnight with a friend."

"I don't want you lying to your family about us," he said.

"But you also don't want me telling them the truth about us, either," she pointed out, lifting her hand to his chin. "That makes it kinda tough, so I told her the truth when I said I might be staying with a friend. You are my friend, aren't you?" she asked, leaning toward him and pulling his head down to hers. "A very, very good friend, right?" she asked and he kissed her.

Abby fell asleep just before ten o'clock, which told him she was continuing to burn the candle at both ends. He'd have to wake her up to fuss at her, though, and she looked so tired he couldn't bring himself to do it. He picked her up and carried her to his bed. She semi-awakened then immediately fell back asleep. Cade slid into the other side of his bed and tried to remember the last time a woman had spent the entire night. His house was his private domain, so he rarely invited a woman to stay longer than an evening. He looked at the outline of her feminine form beneath the covers and knew she was naked underneath. It wouldn't take much for him to want to wake her and make love to her. He knew she wouldn't protest, either. He couldn't remember a woman who had matched his sexual appetite, but Abby did.

He couldn't explain it and sure as hell didn't want to overthink it, but he liked seeing Abby in his bed. She was the last thing he saw before he fell asleep and the first thing he saw when he awakened the next morning. Sometime during the night, she'd snuggled up against him. Her legs were laced through his and one of his arms was curled around her waist. Her eyelids were fluttering and she blinked as her eyes opened as if she weren't sure where she was.

"You're here with me," he said. "In my bed."

"I was getting there," she said. "I'm not always speedy quick in the morning. I don't remember coming into your bedroom," she said, lifting her head to glance around. "I haven't spent a lot of time here before, so I was curious…"

"You didn't get here under your own steam. I carried you," he said.

She looked at him in surprise. "Well, darn, I wish I hadn't missed that." She gave a sheepish smile. "I must have fallen asleep very early. Sorry."

"It wasn't that early," he said and lifted a finger to her nose. "If you're nine years old."

She swatted his hand away. "Thanks a lot. I was a regular box of Cracker Jack last night, minus the popcorn and the toy."

He laughed. "You made up for it before," he said and pulled her against him. "And today you're all mine."

When Abby finally looked out the window, she saw that it had snowed several inches during the night. So much for another motorcycle ride. Not today. They still managed to share a glorious day without leaving Cade's property. After breakfast, she joined him in his workshop as he tinkered with the motorcycle of a friend who had asked him to pimp it out. During the afternoon, he watched part of a college game while she put the finishing touches on her brief PowerPoint presentation. Afterward they went outside and tossed the ball with Stella. The dog couldn't get enough of the game.

When it began to turn dark, they went inside and ordered pizza.

"You're quiet," Cade said after a few moments of silence. "And you're not eating much of the pizza."

"I hate to see the day end," she admitted. Her stomach was clenching at the prospect of returning home and having to pretend that she still wasn't involved with Cade. Plus, the day had been so wonderful and they hadn't done anything monumental. They'd just been together.

"Me, too," he said. "But it will be easier this way if we don't have other people knowing our business."

"I guess," she said.

She saw him stiffen slightly. "You don't agree?"

"Well, I'm one of six children. My mother is all wrapped up in planning Laila's wedding, so I'm not sure she has any time to think twice about who I'm dating as long as he's not a recently released convict."

He chuckled. "I guess I could pass muster on that one. I just don't want to deal with the gossip and uninvited opinions. I don't like people talking about my private business."

"Except when you asked Laila to marry you in front of the whole town," she said, because it popped out of her mouth before she could bite her tongue. She bit her lip instead—way too late.

"That was strictly a moment of insanity invoked by a combination of a stupid discussion with my brothers, whiskey and the fact that I'd recently turned thirty," he said.

Abby gaped at him and covered her mouth. "You were having an age crisis?"

"I figured she probably was, too, since she's the same age as me. I figured I need to start a family sometime. May as well be sooner than later."

Cade could start a family with her, Abby thought, but although he had come around to seeing her as a lover, he didn't seem to view her as a viable option as a wife. The knowledge stung, but her ego had taken a beating more than once with Cade. "So that was a phase," she said. "You're not interested in having a family anymore."

"I didn't say that, but it's got to be the right time with the right person," he said.

A stab of pain shot through her. She'd already hinted that Cade could have what he wanted with her, but he seemed determined not to hear her. She refused to beg. "I hope you find exactly what you're looking for."

He blinked at her response. "What does that mean?"

"Exactly what I said. I think people get into relationships to meet different needs. We all have to figure out who can really meet our needs and who can't," she said and picked up her slice of pizza and prayed she would be able to swallow the bite she took.

Cade seemed more thoughtful than usual during the next hour. He watched her carefully. "I'm thinking you're going to have another busy day tomorrow since you played hooky today."

"You're thinking right," she said, mentally reviewing her insane schedule.

"How's Monday since you'll be busy Tuesday night?" he suggested.

She was impressed that he remembered her standing ROOTS commitment, but didn't allow herself to get too worked up over it. "Monday is better. What did you have in mind?" she asked.

"I'll come up with something better than Monday-night football. Will that work?" he asked.

"Yes. I love surprises," she said.

"It's a good thing one of us does because I hate them," he muttered, then pulled her against him. "What's going on in that pretty head of yours?" he demanded.

"You mean you can't read my mind? I would have sworn that was one of your superpowers," she joked.

"You must have me confused with someone else," he said.

"Nope," she said, shaking her head. "I would swear it was you."

"Well, you're wrong, and I've noticed you still haven't told me what's going on in your brain," he said.

"Good for you," she said, still not revealing her thoughts and feelings. "Observant, too." She lifted her hands to his shoulders and sighed. "When are you going to stop talking and kiss me?"

Between the impending holidays, her cousins' upcoming double wedding and Laila's wedding planning, things at the Cateses' household were moving at a fever pitch. Her sisters were busy with their jobs and social lives, and it always seemed as if one or two of them were moving in or out of the house. Her brother, who still lived at home, provided ample companionship for her father since they were both football freaks and her brother would choose to root for the team opposing her father's choice just to up the ante.

All the busyness made Abby wonder if anyone would really notice if she were gone for a few days, or more. A tempting thought when she daydreamed about taking a trip with Cade... As if that would happen. Maybe in her next life.

On Sunday, her mother encouraged all the kids to go to church. "It won't hurt you. You may even learn something," she'd always said.

Abby often enjoyed the worship service on Sunday morning. It was a quiet slice of time that offered her the opportunity to calm down and remember what was important. Today, however, as she sat with her mother, father, Laila and Jackson, she found herself checking her watch and resisting the urge to squirm. Just two weeks away from Thanksgiving, the sermon topic focused on sharing with both friends and those less fortunate. The pastor pointed out that even though our friends may not seem to need anything, many of us keep our vulnerabilities hidden. He also said that we should especially keep people in mind who have suffered losses during the holidays.

Abby couldn't help thinking of Cade. People thought of him as the man on whom everyone could depend. He was, but Abby had caught a glimpse of the pain of loss he suffered, pain he rarely let anyone see. It frustrated her that he would only let her so close when she was certain she could make some of his pain go away.

Even though he clearly had passion for her, she knew he didn't view their relationship as long-term, and that hurt her every time she thought about it. Something inside her kept her from giving up just yet. During the last hymn, she thought about how to help Cade through the holiday season. Christmas was right around the corner and she wanted him to feel joy instead of dread.

After church, she helped her mother put a big Sunday lunch on the table. Roasted chicken with vegetables, mashed potatoes and biscuits. Her entire family, along with Jackson, made it for the meal.

Abby's father gave a quick grace, and a second after he said "Amen," her brother was reaching for the mashed potatoes.

"I'm glad all of you were able to join us for lunch," Abby's mother said. "I'm sorry you missed church. The minister gave an excellent sermon. Don't you agree, Abby?"

Abby hated being put on the spot, especially when her mother was using her as the example, especially when she was not the least bit perfect. "Very good sermon. The minister reminded us to be generous and thoughtful to everyone because we don't always know when people are suffering. Mom, you and Dad have been such good examples in this area, I'm sure the rest of us will be thinking about this." She searched for a change of subject and glanced at Laila. "How are the wedding plans coming?"

"I can't believe all the details," she said. "It's not just choosing my dress. It's also choosing the bridesmaids' dresses and what the men will wear, the decorations for the church, what the theme will be."

"Vegas sounds like a great theme to me," Jackson muttered. "Eloping."

Abby's mother gasped. "Don't you dare think of it."

"Too late for thinking," Jackson said. "But don't you worry, Mama Cates. I want everyone to know Laila is off the market."

Everyone at the table except Abby laughed. Jackson's comment was in stark contrast to Cade's determination to keep his relationship with her a secret. One more little stab, but Abby brushed it aside.

Speed-cleaning the dishes and kitchen after the meal with a couple of her sisters, Abby mentally planned her afternoon and evening.

"You sure are quiet," Jordyn, one of her sisters, said as she dried a pot.

"And you're cleaning like a bat out of you-know-where," Jasmine agreed, as she dried a pan. "What's the rush? Aren't you gonna hang around for the football game?"

"Not today," Abby said. "I have too much to do. I'm behind on my schoolwork."

"Well, don't work too hard," Jordyn said, shooting her a look of concern. "You're looking a little thin and rough. Circles under your eyes."

"If it were anyone but you, I'd wonder if you were lovesick," Jasmine said just as Laila walked into the kitchen.

"Lovesick?" Laila echoed. "Who's lovesick?"

"No one," Abby said firmly. "I've just got a lot of schoolwork to do. Add that to working at the community center and ROOTS and I'm swamped."

"Hmm," Laila said, clearly unconvinced.

"Like I said," Jasmine repeated. "I'd think you were lovesick if I didn't know you better. You've always been more into your grades than dating."

"And you've always been more into dating than anything else," Abby said with a laugh.

Jasmine swatted at her with the towel, but Abby successfully dodged her sister. "I gotta run. Hope you guys win your bets this time."

"Fat chance," Jordyn said with a mock scowl. "Brody almost always manages to win."

Abby headed for her bedroom to gather her laptop and books. Just as she turned around, Laila appeared in the doorway. "Lovesick?"

Abby's stomach sank. She really didn't want to have this discussion. "Not me," Abby said. "I don't have time to be lovesick."

"But Jazzy had a point. You look like you've lost weight and you have circles under your eyes," Laila said. "I can't help thinking Cade is responsible."

"Cade is not responsible. You know I have a crazy schedule," Abby told her, grabbing her coat from the back of her chair, mentally scolding herself for almost forgetting it. She needed to get her head together. She was far too distracted.

"I also know you're crazy for Cade," Laila said.

"So what if I am?" Abby tossed back at her sister. "You don't quiz Jazzy about all her boyfriends. Why me?"

Laila hesitated. "Because you're different," she said. "Your heart is softer. I'm afraid you could really get hurt."

Her sister's concerns slid past her defenses and Abby fought the sting of tears in her eyes. She dumped her stuff on the desk and wrapped her arms around Laila in a hug. "I'm lucky to have a sister who cares so much about me, but you can't stop this. You can't keep me from getting hurt. This isn't the same as when I was learning to ride a bike and I scraped my knees. I can't turn away from the most amazing man in the world."

Laila groaned. "Oh, no. You really do have it bad."

Abby pulled back and forced a tiny laugh from the back of her tight throat. "Well, it's about time, isn't it?" she asked. "However it turns out, I'll survive. I've got the backbone of a Cates."

Laila sighed. "That's true. I just hate—"

"Stop," Abby said. "Be happy for me. When I'm with Cade, I'm happier than I ever dreamed possible."

Laila gave a slow nod. "But if you need anything from a hug to a place to stay for the night, you let me know."

"I will. Thanks," Abby said. "Now, I've really got to go."

"And don't forget to eat," Laila yelled as Abby flew out the door.

* * *

That night at the library, Abby typed notes on her laptop for two more papers with a deadline before Thanksgiving. She took a sip from a bottle of water as she scanned one of her research books for more facts pertinent to her topic. She'd been so distracted by her time with Cade that she'd slipped up and forgotten about these papers. Plus she'd checked on Katrina today just before her mother showed up for a parental visit. That situation was looking up since Katrina's mother had kicked her boyfriend out of her house and life.

She scratched a note on her notebook and decided to look for another reference. Glancing at the time on her cell phone, she winced. The library closed at midnight and it was already ten-thirty. She searched for a couple more titles that looked promising and headed back to the section that held those books. "Not that, not that, not that," she murmured then found one of her books. "There you are."

"Exactly. There you are," a male voice said from behind her.

Abby swung around to find Daniel standing just a few feet away from her. "Oh, you startled me."

"Gotta keep a girl like you off balance to keep you interested."

Except, she had never been interested, she thought, irritated, as she turned back to the bookshelf. "I really can't chat tonight, Daniel. I've got to find one more book to make some notes."

"You're always busy, Abby. You need to take a break.

You know what they say. All work and no play is bad for your health."

"My health is fine. It will be a lot better when I get through this semester," she muttered as she surveyed the shelves.

Daniel stepped between her and the shelves she was searching. "C'mon, Abby. I've been chasing you for weeks. What's it take to get your attention?"

She noticed the smell of alcohol on his breath and her irritation intensified. "Daniel, I told you I don't have time for this tonight. I don't have time for this at all. I'm not interested in you," she said bluntly. Surely that would make him leave.

"Why not?" he asked, moving toward her, so that she backed against the opposite shelf. "Your friends tell me you need to get out more. You're not involved with anyone." He lowered his head. "I think we could be good together. Very good," he said as he lowered his mouth.

Shocked, Abby turned her head and tried to step away, but Daniel closed his arms around her. "You ought to give me a chance. Just one. I could change your mind."

"Let me go, Daniel," she said, her heart beating with a combination of surprise and fury.

"You smell so good," he said. "I've had dreams about you."

"Daniel!" she yelled, not wanting to alert the entire library over his foolish behavior, but he had crossed over the line.

He slid his mouth over her forehead.

"That's it. I warned you," she said and jerked her knee sharply upward into his groin.

Daniel yelped in pain and doubled over. His whimper made her feel sorry for him, for about a half of a second then her anger came back full throttle.

"What the hell did you do that for?" he asked. "I was just trying to give you a little kiss."

"I didn't want a little kiss," she told him. "I didn't want any kisses from you, and if you ever put your paws on me or anyone else I know in the future, I'm calling the police. When I say no, I mean no. And here's a news flash, that goes for all women. Do you understand me?"

He looked behind her, still grimacing. "Yeah, me and everybody else," he said and limped past her.

Abby whirled around and found at least twenty students, along with the librarian, staring at Daniel, then her. Her face flamed with embarrassment. She made a habit of not calling attention to herself, and to have everyone observing her in this situation was, oh, humiliating. She cleared her throat. "Sorry for the interruption. I, uh, need to get back to work."

Chapter Ten

Another jam-packed day. Abby worked with the kids at the community center, went to two classes, worked more on her two papers and squeezed in a little surprise shopping for Cade. She would have been more excited about her purchases, one of which was burning a hole in her pocket, if she hadn't gotten a late start for his house because her mother had phoned her cell to ask her to pick up some groceries.

She pulled into his driveway and bolted out of the car. Before she could make it up the steps to his porch, he opened the door and leaned against the doorjamb. "Well, well, well, if it isn't the nutcracker herself."

Abby blinked at him and her mental to-do list fell into a pile of dust. "Nutcracker?" she said. "What are you talking about?"

"I'm talking about your new nickname," he said.

Confused, she walked up the steps, noticing a couple sleds propped against the house. Her gaze was drawn back to Cade, and she lifted her shoulders. "What do you mean?"

"As of last night, there are stories going around that a young man named Daniel Payne suffered bodily injuries that you inflicted," Cade said. "Stories I'm certain are not true. Because you would never let a guy get to the point of no return in the college library."

Anger soared through her. "He walked into that library past the point of no return. He'd been drinking. I told him I wasn't interested and never would be, but he wouldn't stop. Crowded me against one of the bookcases. I yelled. I warned, but he wouldn't listen. There was only one thing left to do."

"Did it occur to you to call me?" he asked, something dark flicking through his blue gaze.

"I didn't have my cell phone on me when I was reaching for the book on abnormal psychology. It was very embarrassing. By the time I stopped yelling, a crowd of people were watching and listening. For a minute there, I was afraid I might get banned from the library, but this was not my fault. I have *not* encouraged that guy in any way."

"You still should have called me," he said, scowling at her.

"I told you I didn't have my phone," she said.

"Afterward. You should have called me afterward.

You had to be shaken up and I could have paid this guy a visit to make sure he didn't bother you again," he said.

She felt a rush of warmth at Cade's protectiveness. "That's nice of you," she said softly. "But I don't think there's any danger of him coming anywhere near me again."

"He better not or he's going to have to answer to me," Cade said, pulling her inside his foyer. He opened the closet door and grabbed a hat.

"There's no need to get physical, Cade. You're a lot bigger than he is. You could squash him with one of your feet," she said.

"Look who's talking about not getting physical, *nutcracker,*" he said. "And I've rarely needed to resort to violence in my life. I'll just reason with the guy."

Her stomach began to lurch. Abby had tried not to think about the incident, but down deep it really had bothered her. She knew, based on her studies, that she would have to work through it sooner or later, but later just sounded better to her right now.

"Can we talk about something else? It's not a happy subject for me," she said.

His gaze softened. "Sure, and I have just the thing to take it off your mind," he said, pulling on the hat he held in his hand then following up with his gloves. "We're going sledding."

"Now?" she asked, the idea appealing to her in a surprising way.

"Now," he said. "The hill behind my brother Dean's place is perfect."

"Aren't you worried he'll see us and ask questions about you and me?" she asked.

"Dean knows about you and me," he said, guiding her out the door.

She gaped at him. "He does?"

"Yeah, I told him about it a couple weeks ago. He knows not to discuss it," he said and grabbed the sleds.

Abby was so stunned she didn't know what to say, until a thousand questions entered her mind. *Exactly what did you tell Dean? How much does he know? Two weeks ago? You were still saying I was too young then. Did you tell him you've fallen desperately in love with me and can't live without me?* She rolled her eyes at the last one because she knew the answer to that. *No and no.*

Within an hour, she felt seven years old again. Flying down a snow-covered hill shrieking with joy. Cade dared her to race him. She won once. He won the second time. Then he double-dared her to ride down the hill on his back. Unable to resist, she joined him and they took a tumble in the snow.

"Are you okay?" he asked, his voice anxious as he rolled her from her front side to her back in the snow. "I must have hit some ice."

"I'm fine," she said and started to laugh. "I'm going to be so wet by the time we get back to your house." She laughed again. "And it's all your fault because you are a reckless sled driver."

He frowned with consternation. "I'm not reckless. I just hit some ice. Are you sure you're okay?"

"Fine except for all the snow that's gone all the way down my neck to my back. I never dreamed that perfect Cade could be reckless," she teased.

He looked as if he were trying to be stern with her, but her giggles must have gotten to him. "Sit up, so you don't get any more snow down your sweater," he said, pulling her up. "Look at you. You've got snow all in your hair. You're a mess," he said, shaking his head.

"All your fault, Mr. Reckless," she said and smiled up at him. "I have an early Christmas present for you."

He looked at her in confusion. "Christmas? We've got a whole month to go," he said.

"You wouldn't know that by your display window at Pritchett & Sons," she said.

"True," he said. "So what's this Christmas present? A lump of coal?" he asked with a wary expression.

"Nope," she said and pulled a mistletoe packet out of her pocket. She lifted it above her head. "Oops. Kiss me quick or it's bad luck."

He shook his head and snatched the mistletoe from her. "Trust me, you don't need mistletoe for me to kiss you." He lowered his head and his warm lips took the cold away from her within mere seconds. As he deepened the kiss, her temperature heated up and she wrapped her arms around his neck. She loved his strength. She loved his wisdom and sense of humor. Being with him made her feel so much more than happy. She couldn't think of one word to describe all the ways he affected her. Abby kissed him with all her heart and passion.

Cade responded. A moment later, he finally pulled back, his eyes dark with wanting. "We'd better head back to the house or I'm going to strip you and we're going to give my brother an eyeful. And I would never hear the end of it."

Cade led the way back to his house and they both stomped the snow from their boots before they stepped inside. He glanced at Abby and spotted her teeth chattering and her blue lips from the cold and swore.

"Why didn't you tell me you were freezing?" he asked, pulling off her gloves and coat. "Hold on to me while I help you ditch these boots."

"It wouldn't have done any good. We still had to walk back to your house. It's no big deal. I'll warm up. By next week," she said, smiling through her chattering teeth.

He chuckled despite himself. He didn't like being responsible for her getting this cold. He was surprised at how protective of her he felt. When he'd heard about that Daniel guy molesting her at the library, he'd wanted to go after him but, from what he'd heard, the guy was planning on leaving town for a while. Good riddance, Cade thought and gave up on pulling off the rest of Abby's soggy clothes in the foyer. She needed warm water. He ditched his own jacket and boots.

"Here we go," he said, picking her up in his arms and carrying her down the hall.

"What are you doing?" she asked.

"You need a hot shower," he said, carrying her into

the bathroom. He turned on the jets to the shower then pulled off the rest of her clothes and his. "Ready?" he asked, already distracted by her naked body. It felt as if it had be aeons since he'd made love to her.

He hauled her into the shower and she shrieked. "Are you trying to scald me to death?"

Cade dialed the temperature back a little bit and pulled her against him. She was still cold. He pressed his mouth against her shivering mouth and she put her arms around him as she sank into the kiss. He felt a couple of chatters, but he knew he'd knocked off the worst of the chill when she sighed against his mouth. Her sigh said so much. If her sigh could talk, it would say she trusted him and wanted him. Her sigh said she was already feeling pleasure, but there was more to come. That sigh coupled with her naked body against his was the most wicked and wonderful sensation he'd ever had.

"You can turn up the water temperature now," she said.

He liked the way she heated up, he thought, and he had every intention of making her blood boil with pleasure. Lowering his mouth to her again in a deep, wet kiss with the water streaming over them, he lowered his hands to her breasts, focusing on her responsive nipples.

Abby made a sexy sound and wriggled against him, making him stiff with wanting her. This time, he wanted to make her want and wait. This time he wanted to make her crazy. He lowered one of his hands between her silky thighs and found her warm and wet. He continued to stroke and she began to wiggle against him.

"Cade, I want you," she whispered. "I want you inside me."

"Soon," he promised and dipped his lips to her breasts, taunting her nipples then sliding lower and lower.

Mere minutes later, her body flexed and she climaxed, letting out a high-pitched moan of satisfaction. Taking her with his mouth had nearly put him over the edge. The ability to wait burned to cinders. He picked her up and with her back propped against the tile wall, he took her.

Her sexy gaze burned into his with each stroke he took and somehow in the middle of taking her, he felt as if she had taken him.

After they got out of the shower, Cade wrapped Abby in his big terry-cloth robe and pulled on a pair of jeans and a sweater. "Soup and sandwiches okay with you?" he asked as he pulled from the refrigerator the premade deli sandwiches he'd bought from the grocery store on the way home.

"Perfect. You want me to heat the soup?" she asked, walking into the kitchen. She pulled the foot of the turkey still hanging in his kitchen.

"Gobble, gobble, gobble," said the electronic voice.

Then she pulled it again. "I didn't want him to feel neglected," she said to Cade.

"He hasn't been," Cade assured her. "His foot is

pulled every morning and every evening when I get home from work. Whether he needs it or not."

She gave a low chuckle. "Glad you're taking care of him." She glanced through his cupboard and pulled out a can of soup and poured it into a pot on the stove. "You really do cook like a bachelor, don't you?"

"How's that?" he asked, unwrapping the deli sandwiches and putting them on paper plates.

"I mean you don't cook anything like chicken or soup or stew," she said.

"I cook barbecue pork. Does that count?" he asked.

"On the grill?" she asked.

"Yeah."

"If it's on the grill it doesn't count for real cooking. The grill is great, and I love food cooked on the grill, but sometimes you have to turn on the oven," she said.

He glanced down at the petite woman with wet, mussed hair and big brown eyes who was trying to give him instructions on cooking. He knew that she could cook circles around him. "That's when I turn on the microwave," he said.

"Good for you," she said and laughed.

A few moments later, the soup was heated. She served it with some crackers she found and they sat at the table. "Bean 'n' bacon soup. Excellent choice," he said.

"It's not rocket science. You could have done the same thing," she said. "All it takes is a can opener, a pan and a stovetop."

"That's two steps too many for me," he said, lifting another spoonful of soup to his mouth.

She laughed. "Well, I'm glad I could help out."

He looked into her amused brown eyes and watched her take a bite of her sandwich and felt something inside him ease. What was happening to him? When had canned soup and deli sandwiches felt like a gourmet dinner with Abby sitting across from him.

She met his gaze and glanced away then back at him. "What's wrong? Is there mustard on my chin or something?"

"No. I was just thinking how pretty you are," he said.

Her cheeks flushed. "Thank you. After being hounded by my sisters for looking too thin and having circles under my eyes, that's very nice to hear."

He frowned and studied her. "Now that you mention it," he began.

She shook her head. "Don't you start," she said. "The circles are temporary because of the increased schoolwork at this time of the semester."

"Plus there's the matter of you spending all your extra time with me. I don't want to keep you from your schoolwork," he said.

"Oh, please do," she joked.

"Really, Abby. You're too close to let anything get in your way. Including—" He broke off when his house phone began to ring. "That doesn't happen very often," he said. "Everyone who knows me calls my cell." He paused for a moment then let the call go to voice mail. "What were we talking about?"

"The Jacuzzi you're planning to install," she said.

He chuckled, although the image of Abby naked in a tub of bubbling water was all too appealing. "I've actually thought about it, but never got around to it…"

The phone rang again and he frowned. "Maybe I should check it," he said, rising from the kitchen table. He glanced at the caller ID and felt as if he'd been punched. He immediately picked up the phone.

"Cade Pritchett," he said and waited.

The silence stretched for one, two, three seconds. "Cade, this is Marlene, Dominique's mom."

"Hello," he said. "How are you?"

"Bill and I are doing well. We're actually in Montana visiting some relatives. We wondered if we could drop by and see you tonight," the woman said.

Cade nearly choked on the next breath he drew. "Tonight?" he asked, glancing at Abby, sitting at the table in his robe. She shot him an inquiring glance.

"I know it's short notice, but I think it's important. We won't stay long," she promised.

Hearing the twinge of desperation in the woman's voice, Cade felt compelled to respond. "Okay. I'm finishing up dinner. When do you think you'll be here?"

"In fifteen minutes or less. And we've already eaten, so you don't need to feed us. See you soon," she said.

Cade hung up the phone and stared at it.

"Can you give me a vowel?" Abby asked after a long moment of silence.

"Dominique's parents are coming. They'll be here in less than fifteen minutes."

Abby gaped at him and dumped her spoon in her soup. "Oh, wow, I need to get out of here," she said, rising form her chair. "But we forgot to put my clothes in the dryer, didn't we? Darn," she said. "I could borrow something from you if I wrapped it around me twice."

He chuckled at the image. "Not necessary. You can stay here. We'll throw your clothes in the dryer now."

"I'm not greeting your former girlfriend's parents in your robe," she told him.

"I wasn't suggesting that. You could finish your sandwich in my robe and watch the television in there."

"Oh, hide out in your room," she said. "That could work."

"There's no need for you to hide," he said, frustrated that their evening was being interrupted by people who had held him responsible for the death of their daughter when his biggest crime had been loving her. "If you want to meet them, I'm fine with it."

"I'm not," she said and picked up her plate. She pressed her lips together and looked at him in sympathy. "Good luck, Cade," she said and gave him a kiss. Then she skedaddled toward his bedroom and closed the door behind her.

Cade raked his hand through his hair, wondering why the Gordons had chosen this time to visit him after all these years. His appetite gone, he dumped his soup in the sink and put the remainder of his sandwich in the fridge. He threw Abby's clothes in the dryer and the doorbell rang. Stella barked and ran to the door. Cade brought up the rear and opened the door to the mother and father of the woman he had once planned to marry.

"Hi," Marlene said and timidly stepped inside. "I'm sorry this is such short notice."

Bill extended his hand. "Pritchett," he said with a nod. "Nice to see you. You're looking good."

"Thanks, Bill. Come on in, both of you. Can I get you something to drink?"

"Oh, we won't be staying that long," Marlene said, making him curious as hell. The Gordons looked a little worn around the edges considering their age. Cade supposed he couldn't blame them. They'd had two children and one had died way before she should have.

"How's Bill, Jr.?" Cade asked.

"Doing very well," Marlene said. "He's working for a computer company about an hour away from here. He got married two years ago and he and his wife had a baby six months ago. She's gorgeous."

"Looks like Dominique at that age," Bill said.

Cade's gut tightened. "That's gotta be great for you two," Cade said. "Come into the den."

The two Gordons did as he asked and sat gingerly on the sofa. Silence stretched between them for a long moment.

Bill cleared his throat and adjusted the collar of his coat jacket. "The reason we wanted to see you is because Marlene and I realized we were hard on you when Dominique died."

"We weren't just hard on you," Marlene said. "We weren't fair."

"Dominique was determined to go to California during her break and nothing was going to stop her, even you," Bill said. "You probably knew that. Even if you didn't, you knew what kind of nature Dominique had. She needed to travel every now and then. It was in her blood. She probably got it from me. I went into the air force to see the world."

"We would have done everything to keep her alive, and we believe you would have, too, but who could have predicted that terrible accident?" Maureen asked with a shudder. "We'll never get over the loss, but holding you responsible was wrong and cruel. You were grieving for her, too."

"But we couldn't see that because we were hurting too much," Bill said, lacing and unlacing his fingers.

"So, we're here to apologize," Maureen said. "We were wrong to blame you. We hope you'll forgive us. More important, we hope you don't hold yourself responsible for Dominique's death."

Cade was stunned by all the Gordons were telling him. "I don't know what to say except that I still miss Dominique's presence in my life."

Maureen bit her lip and reached out to pat his hand. "We know you do. Because of that, we'd like to give you the necklace she wore. I believe you gave it to her," Mrs. Gordon said as she pulled a small box from her purse and handed it to Cade.

Cade opened the box to the diamond-accented sparkler pendant he'd given Dominique all those years ago.

He'd told her she was a firecracker and that she lit up his life. The memory squeezed his chest again.

"This was a perfect example of her personality. She was a dynamo. That's one of the reasons we felt such a void when she died," Bill said. "I couldn't stand it. So we moved back to California and tried to make ourselves feel better."

"In some ways, it helped to move away," Marlene said.

"In others, it didn't. How do you explain to people you're meeting for the first time that you had the most beautiful daughter in the world and she would have accomplished amazing things if she hadn't died way too young?"

Cade nodded. "I hear you," he said, his mind suddenly flooded with images of Dominique.

Bill took a deep breath. "We'll never stop missing her," he said.

"Never," Marlene agreed. "But Dominique wouldn't want us to hold a grudge. She would want us to get as much out of life as possible. She would want the same for you, Cade."

Cade felt jolted by Marlene's last comment. "I'm living. I miss her like you do, but I'm living."

"Did you ever get married?" Marlene asked gently.

"Marlene," Bill said. "That's none of our business."

Marlene extended her hand to Cade's again. "Well, I just want to tell you, Cade, that I hope you will find another woman to love. You have a lot to offer and it shouldn't be stuck in the past." She took a deep breath.

"That's all I have to say except to thank you for being so good to Dominique. You were a solid, stable force that made her feel safe enough to fly. You were exactly what she needed at that time in her life."

Cade took in Marlene's words, but he would have to digest them later.

"We should leave now," Bill said to Marlene. He stood and helped his wife to her feet. "Thank you for seeing us. Thank you for being a good man to our daughter and to us," he said and shook Cade's hand again.

"God bless," Marlene said and threw her arms around his neck. "God bless and good night," she said and the two of them left his house.

Cade stared after them, looking at the tire tread marks their vehicle left in the snow. The words from both of the Gordons felt as if they jumbled together in his head. What did all this mean? Did it mean anything? He rubbed the necklace he'd given Dominique all those years ago between his fingers. He felt his lungs constrict. What was he supposed to do with this? As much as he'd loved Dominique, he didn't carry anything of hers around on a daily basis. Nothing material, that is. Her attitude about life had often haunted him. He'd been more practical. She'd enjoyed the unexpected. She'd looked for the magic. Cade didn't believe in magic. But surprises—lately he was changing his mind about those. Or maybe it was Abby who was changing his mind.

The dryer buzzed, signifying the end of the cycle,

and Abby stepped outside the bedroom. "All clear?" she asked in a hushed voice.

When he nodded, she walked toward him, searching his face. "Did it go okay?"

He gave a slow nod. "Yeah. Better than I expected," he said and rubbed his fingers over the pendant in his hand.

Abby glanced down at the necklace. "Did that belong to her?"

"Yeah. I gave it to her when we were dating. They wanted me to have it," he said, still stunned by the conversation he'd had with her parents.

Abby lifted her eyebrows. "Sounds like they had a turnaround."

"Yeah." He paused a moment. "They apologized for blaming me for her death."

"Wow," Abby said. "That's huge." She smiled. "And wonderful. Even though you knew you weren't responsible, it's got to feel great knowing they don't resent you anymore."

He thought about that for a moment. Practically speaking, he'd known he wasn't responsible, but some part of him had thought there must have been something he could have done to prevent Dominique's death. "Sometimes I've wondered if I could have done something to keep her safe. It was my job. It felt like my job, anyway."

"Ohhh," Abby said. "Your superhero complex coming out again. You have the power to save everyone and everything?"

He shot her a sideways glance at her light jab. "It's more that I felt responsible for her."

She nodded. "You were responsible for keeping her safe," she said. "Twenty-four-seven even though you weren't with her and your superpowers are unfortunately limited." She sighed and wrapped her arms around him. "As happy as I am to be with you now, I'm sorry you've had to suffer such a terrible loss."

Her words felt like soothing water on a sore place inside him. He held her close and felt comforted in a way he couldn't remember. Her sweet honesty made a tightness inside him ease. Cade couldn't help wondering if Abby was the one with superpowers.

Chapter Eleven

When Cade went to work the next morning, he felt like a different man. The trees looked prettier, the snow was beautiful, the crisp air felt good to breathe. He hummed along to the country music tune playing on the radio in his SUV. He waved a car in front of him at an intersection. The sun was shining. He would see Abby tonight. Anticipation hummed through him. Today was going to be a good day.

He pulled into the parking lot and got out of his car, ready for a hard, productive day at work followed by an evening with Abby.

"Hey, Cade," his brother Nick said as he walked into the shop. He gave a broad wink. "I hear you've been busy robbing the cradle with another Cates sister."

Cade blinked. Where had Nick heard about him and

Abby? Nick had been on a hunting trip for the past ten days, so this was the first time Cade had seen his brother in a while. Wondering if his other brother, Dean, had been talking, he called for him. "Dean!"

Dean poked his head out from the back room and held up his hands. "It wasn't me. I didn't tell him anything. He went to the Hitching Post last night and apparently the gossip has already started." Dean shot him a sympathetic look. "Sorry, bro."

"I'm not robbing any cradles. Abby's twenty-two." He walked toward the back room. "Welcome back," he added as an afterthought, his mood plummeting. Cade was a private man and hated being the subject of gossip. He was just getting past the fallout from his public proposal to Laila Cates and sure as hell didn't want to stir up anything else.

"So you really are seeing her?" Nick asked, following him to the back room. "It's none of my business, but this isn't a rebound thing because of Laila, is it?"

Cade turned and shot Nick a deadly glance.

"Hey, it's wasn't my idea. One of the waitresses said she wondered if that's what's going on since you lost out on Laila," Nick said.

A month's worth of his patience shot in five minutes, Cade ground his teeth. "Here's a news flash. I don't feel like I lost out on anything with Laila. I'm glad she and Jackson are happy together."

He could tell by his brother's expression that he wasn't convinced. "You've known me a long time. Am

I the kind of man to go out with a woman for the sake of a rebound?"

Nick paused then pressed his lips together in a slight wince. "Sorry. I was just surprised to hear it. Are you serious about her?"

Cade clenched his jaw again. His feelings were nobody's business but his own. "I'm not about to get serious with a woman after two weeks."

"Sure," Nick said. "That makes sense."

Cade sighed and put Nick out of his misery by changing the subject. "So, how was the hunting?"

"Oh," Nick said. "You wouldn't believe the rack on the elk I bagged."

The subject of Abby was blessedly dropped. Cade worked in complete silence without stopping until after lunch and decided to get a breath of fresh air and a cup of coffee and a sandwich to go at the diner. Old man Henson waved at him from a stool as he ate a piece of pie.

Cade placed his order then walked toward him. "How's that ankle?"

"Pretty good. I'm getting around good. Mildred here at the shop has been dropping off some goodies for me after she gets off work. I think she's sweet on me," he said in a lowered voice. "But she's a nice woman. A bit young for me but my Geraldine would approve of her."

Cade smiled. "Good for you," he said.

"I saw your little lady in here this morning. She loves her hot chocolate, doesn't she? Won't touch the coffee. I asked her about you and she said she had seen you a few times." Mr. Henson gave him a nudge. "I knew you would come around. Pretty, sweet and can cook. What's not to like about that?" he asked. "She's a looker and a cooker. You'll do good with her."

"Abby and I aren't serious, so there's no need to be thinking about the future," Cade said.

Mr. Henson shook his finger at him. "Don't you wait too long to get her in your corral. I'll tell you there's plenty of other young bucks right behind you."

Mr. Henson's hearing wasn't the best, so he tended to speak loudly. Cade felt the small crowd in the restaurant watching him. The whispers would start any minute, he realized, and his gut began to churn. "How's that pie?" he asked, pointing toward the pastry on the old man's plate.

"Oh, it's good," Mr. Henson said. "But you know everything here is good."

"How's your truck?" Cade asked. He wanted to provide everyone who was listening with a mundane conversation, so they would turn their attention elsewhere. Away from him.

"Order for Pritchett," the waitress at the register said.

"That's mine," he said to Mr. Henson and slapped the man on the back. "You take care of yourself."

He paid for the order and picked up the bag. "Thanks," he said.

"You're welcome. We all love Abby here. You're a lucky man," the waitress said shyly, then whispered, "I gave you a piece of pie."

Cade clenched his jaw and nodded then left the diner.

* * *

After helping at the community center and going to one of her classes, Abby paid a visit to Katrina since she had just been returned to her mother's apartment. "Everything okay?" Abby asked, sitting across from her on a couch in the modest room.

"It's all good. The foster family was really nice, and they invited me to stop in anytime."

"So you got some new friends out of this," Abby said. "Not bad. You think you would ever visit them?"

"I might," Katrina said, nodding. "They really were nice to me. They always wanted to know where I was, but they were nice."

"And no sign of your mom's boyfriend, right?" Abby asked.

Katrina's eyes darkened. "Ex. My mom's ex. He's gone for good. She promised, and I think she means it. She's talking about dropping one of her jobs so she can spend more time with me."

"That would be great. You know I'm so proud of you, don't you?" Abby said and pulled Katrina into a big hug.

Katrina resisted for half a second then returned the hug. "Yeah. It wasn't fun, but it had to be done. I like that you didn't *make* me do it. You just made me think I deserved to be treated better."

Abby gave her another squeeze then pulled back. "Never, ever forget that," she said.

Katrina met her gaze. "I won't. See ya tomorrow night?"

"I'll be there," Abby said and stood. "Call me if you need anything."

Katrina nodded. "I'll do that."

After going to another class, Abby received terrific grades on an exam and a paper she'd turned in two weeks ago. She was flying high by the time she was scheduled to meet Cade at DJ's for a quick early bite. Just as she entered the eatery, her cell rang. It was Cade.

"Hey," she said. "Everything okay?"

"I decided to pick up ribs and bring them back to the house. Is that okay with you?" he asked.

"Sure, sure," she said, but wondered about something she heard in his voice. "I should be there in about fifteen minutes."

"See you then," he said and hung up.

His tone bothered her, but she had no idea what was wrong. She would ask when she got to his house. The important thing was that they would be together. She'd been looking forward to seeing him since she woke up this morning, she thought, smiling to herself.

Pulling into his driveway, she bounded up the steps, knocked on the door and stepped inside. Stella immediately came to greet her, wagging her tail. "Welcome me here, darlin'," she called. "I've had a crazy-good day and it's just gonna get better."

Cade appeared in the doorway with an inscrutable expression on his face. "What happened during your crazy-good day?" he asked in a subdued tone.

"Are you okay?" she asked, studying him.

"Tell me your good news," he said.

She rubbed Stella's soft, furry head and stepped toward him. "Where do I begin?" she said and looped her arm in his. "I got As on my exam and one of my major papers. Katrina moved back in with her mother and that's looking good. And the best thing is I get to see you." She stood up on tiptoe and pressed her lips against his.

He gave a brief response. "Good for you. Congratulations."

She looked at him in confusion. "Something's wrong. Tell me," she urged.

"Some things happened today that made me start thinking," he said.

"About what?" she asked.

He took a quick breath and narrowed his eyes. "About us."

"What about us?" she asked, his expression making her stomach knot. "Have you been happy when you've been with me?"

"Yeah," he said. "I've been happy."

"That's good, because I've been unbelievably happy. The only thing that would make me happier is if we didn't have to keep it a secret. My feelings for you seemed to be growing exponentially every day. Every time we're together, I feel closer to you. I—" She bit her tongue, but could no longer hold back the words. "I love you, Cade. You're such an incredible man. Being with you is a dream come true for me."

Cade looked at her for a long moment then looked away.

Her heart fell at his lack of response. *Oh, please, Cade, don't bail on me now.*

He lifted one of his hands and cleared his throat. "Sweetheart, you may think you want me. You may think you love me, but you haven't been around me enough to really know that."

She stared at him in disbelief, then shook her head. "Yes, I have. I've known you forever."

"You haven't known me as a man," he said. "Even you would say you've been carrying around a heavy dose of hero worship for a long time."

"And it was valid. You've been a hero to a lot of people. You've been the man that so many people knew they could depend on, especially if they needed help," she said. "I could meet a hundred other men and it wouldn't make any difference to my feelings. I know my own heart."

"Just listen to me. I think we need to slow things down," he said, meeting her gaze.

Shock rushed through her. "Slow down? Now?" She laughed in disbelief. "It's too late for that. I'm in love with you, Cade." She paused and the silence that followed was deafening.

She shook her head. "You can't say it, can you?" She felt as if her world had been turned upside down. "You obviously have feelings for me, but you can't say them. It's just you, me and Stella, and you can't say anything about what I mean to you."

He clenched his jaw and she could see he was wrestling with something inside him. But it looked as if she wasn't on the winning side.

Insidious, ugly doubt crept inside her. Her sister's words of warning played through her mind. Maybe Cade didn't really love her. Maybe he couldn't.

She bit her lip as her chest twisted so tightly it hurt. "I don't know what to say. You can stand up in front of hundreds of people and ask Laila to marry you, but you can't give me any words at all. None," she said and waited through another agonizing silence.

"I need to go," she said, feeling the pressure of tears build behind her eyes. She ran for the door. She stumbled down the steps and blindly climbed into her car. The first sob racked through her and she tried to keep another at bay as she started her car. If she could just get away from his house, off his property, away from him…

She barreled down the driveway, tears falling heedlessly down her cheeks. She swiped at them so she could see to turn onto the road. Abby felt as if her heart was being ripped from her chest. She couldn't remember hurting this much, feeling this much pain. Her throat ached from holding back her sobs. She pulled into a church parking lot and killed the engine of her little car and cried until she wore herself out with her grief.

Gutted from her emotional outburst, she knew this wouldn't be the last time she would cry. Putting her car into gear, she began to drive and hated that Laila's prediction had become true. Cade, her beautiful, wonderful, caring Cade, wasn't capable of giving his heart anymore. Abby had come into his life too late.

Instead of driving home, she found herself heading for Laila's apartment. She couldn't face her family. She really didn't want to face anyone right now, but she thought Laila might understand her feelings. Laila's heart had never been broken, but she'd seen Abby's broken heart coming from a mile away.

She closed her eyes and sighed. Was there any way she could have prevented this? It would have been the same as trying to prevent a blizzard. She debated going to Laila's apartment. Her sister might not even be there. Jackson could be there. Abby almost decided to drive away, but punched her sister's cell-phone number. One ring. Two rings. Three— Abby lifted her finger over the stop button.

"Hey, Abby, what's up?" Laila said.

"Are you busy?" Abby asked.

"No. I was going to meet Jackson for dinner, but he has a special conference call. You want to go somewhere for dinner?"

"I'm not very hungry," Abby said, cursing the waver in her voice.

"Abby, are you okay?" Laila asked, concern threading through her voice. "Where are you?"

"In your parking lot," Abby said, her voice caught between tears and laughter.

"Get your butt up here right now," Laila said. "Or I'll come out there and get you myself."

Her sister's scolding warmed her heart. "Okay. I'm coming, but it's not gonna be pretty."

She made her way to her sister's apartment, and Laila was holding the door open before Abby even arrived. Laila scooped Abby into her arms and ushered her into her apartment. "What happened, sweetie?"

Unable to bear the sweet worry in her sister's gaze, Abby looked down. "You were right," she said, the terrible knot growing in her throat again. "You were right. Cade can't love me," she said and began to sob again.

"Oh, Abby," Laila said and guided her to the sofa and just held her while she cried.

Abby finally felt her tears wane. "Sheesh," she said, taking a deep breath. "You would think I wouldn't have any more water left in me."

Laila gave a soft smile. "Let me fix you a cup of tea."

"I don't really like tea," Abby said.

"You will right now. I'll add a little honey and booze. Lean your head back on the sofa and take some deep breaths."

While Laila made her tea, Abby closed her eyes and felt as if the room were spinning. Laila gave her a cool, damp washcloth for her face then doctored her cup of tea and brought it to her.

"Wait a moment or two then just sip it," Laila said and pushed Abby's hair from her face. "I was so afraid of this happening. You never got involved in the games with guys. You weren't interested in stringing along a bunch of guys just for the fun of it. You were saving your heart for the real thing. I knew that when you decided to love someone, you would love with all your heart. When I first saw you and Cade getting involved, I thought it could be good for both of you. But the more I thought about it, the more I became afraid, because you're so emotional and Cade is not."

"But he is," Abby said. "That's the thing. He's very emotional. He's talked with me about losing his mom and Dominique."

Laila widened her eyes in surprise. "Whoa. Dominique? That surprises me. He was always a clam when it came to that subject."

"He is an emotional man," Abby said. "But I'm afraid you're right that he can't give his heart again." She felt the terrible sensation of tears backing up behind her eyes again and groaned. "Not again. I don't want to cry again."

"Sip your tea," Laila said.

Abby did as Laila instructed.

"And another," Laila said.

Abby took another sip. "This isn't bad."

"The honey and the booze help. Keep on sipping. I wish I could tell you that it's a magic drink and you'll never cry again, but I would be lying," Laila said. "You love too hard for it not to hurt a lot when it doesn't work out. But listen to me," Laila said, dipping her head to look straight into Abby's gaze. "You deserve a man who loves just as hard as you do and nothing less."

"I'm not sure such a man exists," Abby said hopelessly.

"You don't have to think about whether he exists or

not tonight. You just need to know that you deserve a man who can give you all his heart. Now, I'm going to call Jackson and tell him not to come over."

"Oh, no, I don't want to interrupt—"

"You're not interrupting. I can see Jackson tomorrow. You and I will drink spiked tea and watch something stupid on television." She gave Abby another hug. "I'm glad you came to me. It means a lot. Now let me put on some more tea."

Laila provided a much-needed diversion from Abby's misery, and after another cup of tea, Abby had no trouble falling asleep the second her head hit the pillow. When she awakened in the morning, though, her pain hit her first thing. Her impulse was to pull the covers over her head, but she knew she couldn't.

Forcing herself from bed, she took a shower and the water felt like a healing spray on her face and body. Afterward, she walked into the kitchen where Laila was fixing eggs and bacon. "There you are. Good morning, sunshine," she said.

"Yeah, sunshine. That's me," Abby said. "Impressive breakfast."

"Feel the love. You better eat it," she said spooning the food onto a plate. "Orange juice? Coffee? Oh, that's right. You don't drink coffee."

Surprised, Abby took a bite of bacon. "I'm surprised you knew I didn't like coffee," Abby said, sitting down at the kitchen table.

"Why wouldn't I?" Laila asked, joining her at the table. "You're my sister."

"I'm one of six. You can't know the preferences of all of us," she said.

"You'd be surprised. You may think no one notices you, but we're all proud of you. We know you make straight As. We talk about you behind your back and wonder if you're going to be the first one to get an advanced degree."

"I've got to get this one first," she said. "But it's nice to know you're rooting for me even if it's done in secret."

"Right. Now you're going to need a strategy so you don't burst into tears every other hour," Laila said. "You need to keep busy, but also take lots of naps."

"How do you know about this? You've never had a broken heart," Abby said.

"I've gotten close a couple times, but I've nursed a few friends through some terrible breakups. And," she said, putting her hand on Abby's arm, "I couldn't stand it if Jackson and I broke up now. The very thought of it makes my heart stop. It would be too terrible."

Abby nodded, the yawning sadness stretching inside her.

"But you don't have to do it alone. I want you to call me anytime. If you don't call me, I'll harass you. And remember, you have the Cates backbone," Laila said. "Now eat your breakfast. You need nourishment."

Abby left Laila's apartment and went home to change clothes. Thank goodness she had a busy day. She worked at the community center, gave her presentation for class, finished a paper and forced down a sandwich before she left for ROOTS. The girls were wired tonight because Thanksgiving was less than two weeks away. They sorted donated food into bags for families in need. By the end of the evening, all of them were pleased with how much they'd accomplished.

"You guys did great," Abby said. "Tell your parents what you did tonight, and if they could use a bag because growing teenagers eat food like they have holes in their legs, send them over. We're still collecting food."

"You'll be here next week, right?" Katrina asked.

"Absolutely. Wouldn't miss our before Thanksgiving get-together. But I have to tell you I've got a ton of work right now with my classes. So you won't get much sympathy from me if you're not staying on top of your schoolwork," Abby said.

There was a collective groan. "Whatever happened with that guy you liked? When we fixed your makeup and hair so you could get his attention?" Keisha asked.

Abby felt a sudden stab of pain and took a quick breath. "Didn't work out. I guess he wasn't the right one."

"Stupid guy," Keisha said. "You're the best."

"Thanks," Abby said. "I needed that."

Abby successfully made it home, made a cup of herbal tea with a heavy dose of honey and let it cool while she took a shower. She took a few sips and climbed under her bedcovers and cried herself to sleep.

Cade worked around the clock on Tuesday through Wednesday. Work was a solace. He felt as if he'd smashed a butterfly. Every time he closed his eyes, he saw Abby's hurt face. The devastation he'd seen in her gaze, heard in her voice, made him feel like the worst human being on the face of the earth. The truth was that he did have feelings for Abby. The truth was also that he couldn't give Abby what she needed. He'd known that from the beginning and it had only become more clear with each time he'd shared with her.

He never should have given in to his feelings for her, but she'd made him greedy for her passion and lightness. She'd made him want what he hadn't had in too long, maybe what he'd never had.

"Take a break," his father said. "We're all going to the community center to watch the kids do their little show."

"I'm not in the mood," Cade said.

"Well, get in the mood," his father said. "We have to be good examples. The director invited us, so we have to go. You look like hell. Brush your hair, wash your face. Do something to yourself, then come over. It won't last that long."

Cade washed his face, brushed his teeth and tried to avoid looking in the mirror. He had done what he was determined not to do. Hurt Abby.

Pulling on a jacket and putting a hat on his head, he walked over to the community center. It was a cold night and the scent of oncoming snow was heavy in the air. The merchants were mixing Thanksgiving and Christmas lights and decorations in anticipation of the holiday season. As usual, he felt no joy at the season.

Abby would, though. She would find a way to get him to smile, use something like that dang gobbling turkey still hanging in his kitchen or hold some mistletoe over his head.

He tried to shake off the thoughts as he stepped inside the community center to the sound of children singing. Standing in the back, he watched the kids perform their well-practiced show. One little pilgrim forgot his words and he heard Abby give a prompt. His gaze automatically flew in her direction.

The room was more dark than not, so he had to focus to find her, but he did, standing on one side in the front, encouraging the kids. She would be a great mother, he thought. Loving and fun-loving, she would make growing up an adventure, just as she would make marriage an adventure for the right man. She would find him, he knew. The knowledge brought a bitter taste to his mouth.

He stayed through the rest of the show, but left as soon as the audience applauded. He needed to get home. With his mind being tortured nonstop, he needed the escape that sleep could provide.

After arriving home, he turned on the TV to drown out the silence, then downed a peanut-butter sandwich and a glass of milk. The TV quickly annoyed him, so he turned it off. Stella watched him wander around from the den to the kitchen and back. Little bits of Abby mocked him. The turkey hanging in his kitchen, mistletoe she'd hung in three different doorways. It was more painful for him to look at that turkey than it was for him to look at Dominique's necklace.

Craving the need to escape his thoughts of her, he took a shower, praying it would wash thoughts of Abby from his head. He went to bed and tossed and turn then finally fell asleep.

Cade heard the collision and the crunch of metal and glanced behind him. What he saw filled him with horror. Abby's cute little VW was a twisted mess. A truck had ran into her little car just outside his driveway.

His heart pounding in his chest, he raced to help Abby. She had to be okay, he told himself. She had to be. He got to her car and saw her slumped in the seat, unconscious. A trickle of blood slid down the side of her cheek.

"Abby," he yelled at the top of his lungs as he beat on the VW's window. "Abby!"

The sound of his own voice awakened Cade. His body drenched in a cold sweat, he shook his head, still locked in the terrible nightmare where he couldn't get to Abby, where he couldn't help her.

Sucking in deep breaths of air, he blinked his eyes and turned on his bedside lamp. It had been a dream, he told himself. A dream. Still, he reached for his cell phone and his finger hovered over the speed dial for her phone number. He just wanted to hear her voice, to make sure she was okay. That was all he needed.

Reality finally began to penetrate his brain, and he

scolded himself. He needed to get control of his emotions. He was totally out of hand. He was going to have to work harder at reining in his feelings. When he'd let his heart get away from him in the past, it had always led to pain. This time was no different.

On Thanksgiving morning, Cade went to DJ's along with what seemed like everyone else in the community to pack up turkey and rib dinners for the less fortunate. He walked into the diner and nearly walked straight into Abby.

He reached out to steady her, but Abby put up her hands and stumbled backward as if she would do anything to keep him from touching her. The knowledge stabbed at him. "Hey," he said. "How are you doing?"

She bit her lip and didn't meet his gaze. "I'm okay. Busy as usual. Oh, look, there's Austin," she said, gesturing toward a familiar-looking young man.

Cade studied the guy for a few seconds and realized this was the young man who had taken Abby out that night she'd been dressed to thrill. He felt a twist of jealousy even though he knew he had no right.

Abby glanced at one of several sheets of paper she held in her hand. "Austin," she called. "Rose," she said to the Traubs' sister and waved them toward her. "Do you two mind riding together to deliver the dinners? We want to start making deliveries as soon as possible because they're all spread out." Abby paused a moment then gave a slight smile. "Oops, maybe you two haven't met."

"I can take care of that," Austin said and extended his hand. "Austin Anderson. I've seen you around, but was never lucky enough to meet you."

Rose smiled. "Rose Traub. I believe my brothers are better known than I am," she said wryly.

"I can't imagine why," Austin said. "They can't be nearly as pretty."

Rose glanced at Abby. "Thanks for putting me with someone who has a sense of humor. It will make the day go faster."

"Have fun," Abby said to both of them and gave them a sheet of paper. "Here are the names and addresses for your deliveries. Thanks so much for your help."

Cade forced himself to move away from her even though he wanted nothing more than to be close to her, even in this room full of other people. Spending the past week without her had been pure hell. But necessary, he told himself as he joined an assembly line putting together the food boxes. He loaded a box of ribs into each package of food.

The room was full of conversation and purposeful activity. He heard a few people chuckling and wondered when he would feel like laughing again.

Suddenly an unfamiliar young woman approached Zane Gunther, the country music star who had made Thunder Canyon his home and recently fallen in love. "Mr. Gunther, I'm Tania Tuller. Ashley was my sister."

The whole room turned quiet because everyone knew that Zane was fighting a lawsuit over a fan dying at one of his concerts. The tragedy had apparently forced Zane to reconsider his career in the fast lane. The poor guy had been horrified that such a thing could happen at one of his concerts.

"Mr. Gunther, if there's one thing I've learned from my sister's death, it's that none of us knows how long we have here to live our lives. That means we've got to go after our dreams and make the best out of the time we're given. Holding grudges is a waste of precious time. Ashley died going after her dream of seeing her hero. You were her hero," Tania said, her voice breaking.

Zane stepped toward Tania and put his arm around her to support her. Tania leaned against him. "My parents' lawsuit is an idea. Ashley would be horrified by it. Your music was the light of her life. I'm going to try my best to talk my parents out of this lawsuit, and I really believe I can."

Murmurs spread throughout the room like wildfire. Cade watched Zane speak quietly with Tania, but he found Tania's words sticking him like needles. Almost everything she said could have been directed at him. Life is short. He might not be holding on to a grudge, but holding on to fear was just as bad or worse.

He looked at Abby, who was struggling to put on a brave face, but he could tell she was miserable, and he was the cause of it. An overwhelming wave of realization swept over him. Abby was the woman of his dreams. She made him feel as if anything were possible. Being with her gave him the deepest sense of peace and happiness he'd ever dreamed possible.

Hard facts slammed into him. Fear had been holding him back. Fear might be why he wasted so many years dating Laila. Deep down, he knew that spending time with her was safe. He was so scared he would lose Abby that he was pushing her away before he could get hurt. Cade couldn't wait one more minute to talk to her.

Striding across the room, he stood directly in front of her and looked into her sad brown eyes and wanted to kick himself. "I've been a fool," he said. "You've misunderstood my reaction to you and I've been fighting my feelings like a bull in a china shop. I love you so much it freaks me out."

Abby blinked in surprise. "What?"

"Yeah, and I think deep down you suspected it. When I wanted to back off, I confused you. I'm so sorry for that," he said, shaking his head. "I love you so much that the thought of losing you scares me to death."

"But you didn't lose me. You pushed me away."

"I didn't lose you, but I've lost others. What I feel for you is stronger than anything I've ever known before. What if I lost you, too?" he asked, the sound of his voice gruff to his own ears.

"Oh, Cade," she said, stepping into his arms. "I wish you had talked about this with me before. I never want you to suffer like this. Never."

The sensation of her body against his was so sweet he had to catch his breath. "I've been a total hard-headed fool. You're everything I've ever wanted. I just hope you can forgive me."

She bit her lip as if she wasn't sure she could trust

him. That possibility tore at him and he was determined to regain her confidence in him.

"You know that people will talk about us. Are you sure that's not going to bother you? Are you sure you're not going to change your mind?"

"Not in a million years," he said. "Let them talk. The most important thing in the world to me is you."

Cade wasn't given to wild impulses, but Abby brought out all kinds of surprising things inside him. He climbed on top of a table. "Listen, everybody. I love Abby Cates."

A heartbeat of silence passed before the room exploded with applause. Cade jumped off the table and pulled Abby back into his arms. Her face was full of shock and happiness. "Cade?" she said in surprise.

"Better get used to it, Abby. This is the effect you have on me," he said and took her mouth in a kiss for all the world to see.

Epilogue

Abby experienced the most thankful Thanksgiving day in her history. Every time she thought about Cade standing up on that table in DJ's to profess his love for her in front of everyone, she pinched herself to believe it was true. Of course, it helped that everyone in Thunder Canyon wanted to replay the scene with her over and over. Old man Henson chuckled over it every time she saw him, and the servers at the diner thought it was the most romantic thing they'd ever heard. Even her ROOTS girls wanted to hear the story over and over like a fairy tale from when they were little girls.

Her parents had always loved Cade, so they were thrilled, and Laila was pleasantly surprised to hear that Cade had stepped up the way he should. After Thanksgiving, the days passed with the speed of light and suddenly it was time for the Cateses' double wedding.

Cade was taking her to the wedding, of course. They'd spent every possible moment with each other, and both freely admitted, every possible moment just wasn't enough. Abby followed in her mother's footsteps by putting Christmas decoration in every room of Cade's house, including the bathroom. At first Cade had thought it was ridiculous, but she'd heard him humming the Christmas song from a music box she'd placed in his bedroom on more than one occasion.

Although her friend Austin Anderson had originally planned to escort her, he'd graciously bowed out and Abby had heard he was taking Rose Traub.

Abby wore a navy velvet dress in honor of the holiday season, curled her hair and applied her makeup with care. This was the event of the season but, more importantly, she wanted to impress Cade. She wondered if there would ever be a time when she didn't want to impress him and just couldn't imagine it. At the same time, though, Cade made her feel as if she were the most beautiful woman in the world even if it was the end of the day and she knew she looked as tired as she felt.

"Abby!" her father called. "Cade's here."

Abby grabbed her coat and walked into the living room where Cade stood in a dark suit that set off his light hair and blue eyes. All she could do was stare.

"You look amazing," he said.

She laughed breathlessly. "I was just thinking the same thing about you."

"All right, you lovebirds, get on your way. I'm going to have to push my wife out the door soon. Never seen so much primping in my life," her father said. He'd been ready for a half hour.

"What do you expect, Daddy? It's a double wedding in a ballroom. We all want to look our best," Abby said and pressed a kiss on her father's cheek. "We'll see you there."

Cade led her to his SUV and helped her into the car. They talked during the entire ride about how they'd spent their morning. Soon enough, they arrived at the wedding. A line of guests formed, waiting to be seated for the ceremony of two of Thunder Canyon's most beloved couples. Abby could feel the excitement and anticipation in the air.

"Oh, look," she said. "There's Zane Gunther with Jeannette. She looks so pretty."

"Did you hear that the Tullers dropped their lawsuit against Zane?" he asked.

"No," she said. "That's wonderful news."

Cade nodded. "He's started a special foundation in Ashley's honor and he's naming it The Ashley Tuller Foundation."

"He's a good guy. It's amazing how fast he and Jeannette got together. They're already engaged."

"When it's right," Cade said, looking into her gaze, "you know it. And there's no need to waste time."

Her stomach dipped and she squeezed his hand. She stood on tiptoe and whispered in his ear. "I love you more than anything, Cade Pritchett."

He snuck a quick kiss and sighed. "This may be bad timing, but—"

"What?" she asked, confused by the nervous expression on his face.

"Come here," he said, pulling her away from the crowd. He led her to a quiet, private place on the other side of the building. The wind fluttered through his hair, making her want to touch it.

"I had wanted to wait to give this to you for Christmas, but I can't. Everything is right with you. You make me feel more complete, more at peace, more happy than I have in my entire life. I don't want to wait another minute without taking the next step," he said.

Her heart beating like a helicopter's propeller, she stared at him. "What are you talking about?"

Abby watched as Cade knelt down one knee and pulled a small velvet box from his pocket. He opened it and lifted it for her to see a beautiful diamond ring. Abby gasped at the sight of it, but she couldn't keep her eyes off of Cade. Was this really happening? She was certain she was having an out-of-body experience.

"Abby, I love you with all my heart and soul. You are my true soul mate. There is nothing that would make me happier than to spend the rest of my life with you. Will you marry me?"

Abby's hands began to shake. She couldn't believe this was happening. Yes, she'd had a crush on Cade for as long as she could remember, but her crush had grown into a woman's love. Knowing that he wanted her to be his was so powerful she nearly couldn't comprehend it. "Could you repeat that last bit?" she managed in a husky whisper.

Cade stood and pulled her into his arms. "I love you, darlin'. Say you'll be mine forever."

With his arms around her, the reality set in. Cade Pritchett had just asked Abby Cates to marry him. "Yes," she said. "Yes, I will."

Cade placed the ring on her finger and sealed their promise with a kiss that sent Abby around the world. She knew she and Cade had found the love of a lifetime, and they would always cherish each other.

* * * * *

HEART & HOME

Heartwarming romances where love can
happen right when you least expect it.

Harlequin
SPECIAL EDITION

COMING NEXT MONTH
AVAILABLE NOVEMBER 22, 2011

#2155 TRUE BLUE
Diana Palmer

#2156 HER MONTANA CHRISTMAS GROOM
Montana Mavericks: The Texans Are Coming!
Teresa Southwick

#2157 ALMOST A CHRISTMAS BRIDE
Wives for Hire
Susan Crosby

#2158 A BABY UNDER THE TREE
Brighton Valley Babies
Judy Duarte

#2159 CHRISTMAS WITH THE MUSTANG MAN
Men of the West
Stella Bagwell

#2160 ROYAL HOLIDAY BRIDE
Reigning Men
Brenda Harlen

You can find more information on upcoming Harlequin® titles,
free excerpts and more at www.HarlequinInsideRomance.com.

HSECNM1111

REQUEST YOUR FREE BOOKS!

2 FREE NOVELS PLUS 2 FREE GIFTS!

❖ Harlequin®

SPECIAL EDITION

Life, Love & Family

YES! Please send me 2 FREE Harlequin® Special Edition novels and my 2 FREE gifts (gifts are worth about $10). After receiving them, if I don't wish to receive any more books, I can return the shipping statement marked "cancel." If I don't cancel, I will receive 6 brand-new novels every month and be billed just $4.49 per book in the U.S. or $5.24 per book in Canada. That's a saving of at least 14% off the cover price! It's quite a bargain! Shipping and handling is just 50¢ per book in the U.S. and 75¢ per book in Canada.* I understand that accepting the 2 free books and gifts places me under no obligation to buy anything. I can always return a shipment and cancel at any time. Even if I never buy another book, the two free books and gifts are mine to keep forever.

235/335 HDN FEGF

Name	(PLEASE PRINT)	
Address		Apt. #
City	State/Prov.	Zip/Postal Code

Signature (if under 18, a parent or guardian must sign)

Mail to the **Reader Service:**
IN U.S.A.: P.O. Box 1867, Buffalo, NY 14240-1867
IN CANADA: P.O. Box 609, Fort Erie, Ontario L2A 5X3

Not valid for current subscribers to Harlequin Special Edition books.

Want to try two free books from another line?
Call 1-800-873-8635 or visit www.ReaderService.com.

* Terms and prices subject to change without notice. Prices do not include applicable taxes. Sales tax applicable in N.Y. Canadian residents will be charged applicable taxes. Offer not valid in Quebec. This offer is limited to one order per household. All orders subject to credit approval. Credit or debit balances in a customer's account(s) may be offset by any other outstanding balance owed by or to the customer. Please allow 4 to 6 weeks for delivery. Offer available while quantities last.

Your Privacy—The Reader Service is committed to protecting your privacy. Our Privacy Policy is available online at www.ReaderService.com or upon request from the Reader Service.

We make a portion of our mailing list available to reputable third parties that offer products we believe may interest you. If you prefer that we not exchange your name with third parties, or if you wish to clarify or modify your communication preferences, please visit us at www.ReaderService.com/consumerschoice or write to us at Reader Service Preference Service, P.O. Box 9062, Buffalo, NY 14269. Include your complete name and address.

HSE11B

Lucy Flemming and Ross Mitchell shared a magical, sexy Christmas weekend together six years ago. This Christmas, history may repeat itself when they find themselves stranded in a major snowstorm… and alone at last.

Read on for a sneak peek from
IT HAPPENED ONE CHRISTMAS
by Leslie Kelly.

Available December 2011, only from Harlequin® Blaze™.

EYEING THE GRAY, THICK SKY through the expansive wall of windows, Lucy began to pack up her photography gear. The Christmas party was winding down, only a dozen or so people remaining on this floor, which had been transformed from cubicles and meeting rooms to a holiday funland. She smiled at those nearest to her, then, seeing the glances at her silly elf hat, she reached up to tug it off her head.

Before she could do it, however, she heard a voice. A deep, male voice—smooth and sexy, and so not Santa's.

"I appreciate you filling in on such short notice. I've heard you do a terrific job."

Lucy didn't turn around, letting her brain process what she was hearing. Her whole body had stiffened, the hairs on the back of her neck standing up, her skin tightening into tiny goose bumps. Because that voice sounded so familiar. *Impossibly* familiar.

It can't be.

"It sounds like the kids had a great time."

Unable to stop herself, Lucy began to turn around, wondering if her ears—and all her other senses—were deceiving her. After all, six years was a long time, the mind could play tricks. What were the odds that she'd bump into *him*, here? And today of all days. December 23.

Six years exactly. Was that really possible?

One look—and the accompanying frantic thudding of her heart—and she knew her ears and brain were working just fine. Because it was *him*.

"Oh, my God," he whispered, shocked, frozen, staring as thoroughly as she was. "Lucy?"

She nodded slowly, not taking her eyes off him, wondering why the years had made him even more attractive than ever. It didn't seem fair. Not when she'd spent the past six years thinking he must have started losing that thick, golden-brown hair, or added a spare tire to that trim, muscular form.

No.

The man was gorgeous. Truly, without-a-doubt, mouthwateringly handsome, every bit as hot as he'd been the first time she'd laid eyes on him. She'd been twenty-two, he one year older.

They'd shared an amazing holiday season.

And had never seen one another again.

Until now.

Find out what happens in
IT HAPPENED ONE CHRISTMAS
by Leslie Kelly.
Available December 2011, only from Harlequin® Blaze™

Copyright © 2011 by Leslie Kelly.

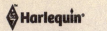

Harlequin®

LAURA MARIE ALTOM
brings you
another touching tale from

When family tragedy forces Wyatt Buckhorn to pair up
with his longtime secret crush, Natalie Poole, and care
for the Buckhorn clan's seven children, Wyatt worries
he's in over his head. Fearing his shameful secret will
be exposed, Wyatt tries to fight his growing attraction
to Natalie. As Natalie begins to open up to Wyatt,
he starts yearning for a family of his own—a family
with Natalie. But can Wyatt trust his heart enough
to reveal his secret?

A Baby in His Stocking

Available December
wherever books are sold!

www.Harlequin.com

HAR75387

Harlequin®

Romance

SUSAN MEIER

Experience the thrill of falling in love this holiday season with

Kisses on Her Christmas List

When Shannon Raleigh saw Rory Wallace staring at her across her family's department store, she knew he would be trouble…for her heart. Guarded, but unable to fight her attraction, Shannon is drawn to Rory and his inquisitive daughter. Now with only seven days to convince this straitlaced businessman that what they feel for each other is real, Shannon hopes for a Christmas miracle.

Will the magic of Christmas be enough to melt his heart?

Available December 6, 2011.

www.Harlequin.com

HR17769